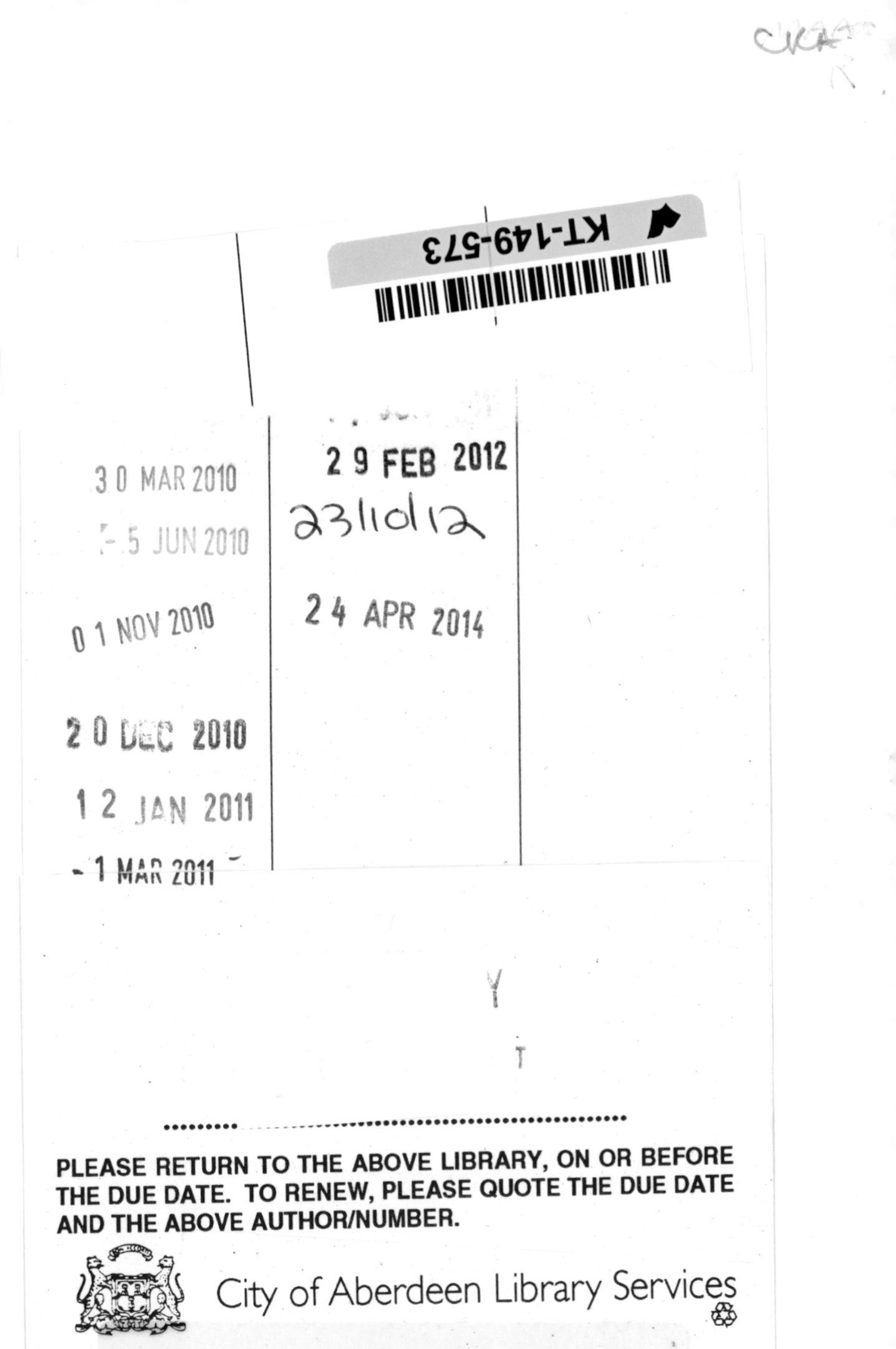

Gunhill

Gunhill

Lauran Paine

THORNDIKE
CHIVERS

This Large Print edition is published by Thorndike Press, Waterville, Maine, USA and by BBC Audiobooks Ltd, Bath, England.
Thorndike Press, a part of Gale, Cengage Learning.

The text of this Large Print edition is unabridged.
Other aspects of the book may vary from the original edition.
Set in 16 pt. Plantin.
Printed on permanent paper.

LIBRARY OF CONGRESS CATALOGING-IN-PUBLICATION DATA

Paine, Lauran.
Gunhill / by Lauran Paine.
p. cm. — (Thorndike Press large print western)
ISBN-13: 978-1-4104-0910-2 (alk. paper)
ISBN-10: 1-4104-0910-4 (alk. paper)
1. Mothers and daughters—Fiction. 2. Ranch life—Colorado—Fiction. 3. Cattle stealing—Fiction. 4. Large type books. I. Title.
PS3566.A34G86 2008
813'.54—dc22 2008021512

BRITISH LIBRARY CATALOGUING-IN-PUBLICATION DATA AVAILABLE

Published in 2008 in the U.S. by arrangement with Golden West Literary Agency.
Published in 2009 in the U.K. by arrangement with Golden West Literary Agency.

U.K. Hardcover: 978 1 408 41295 4 (Chivers Large Print)
U.K. Softcover: 978 1 408 41296 1 (Camden Large Print)

Printed in the United States of America
1 2 3 4 5 6 7 12 11 10 09 08

Gunhill

1

The Reverend James Carmichael had become an ordained minister of the Gospel the year following his discharge from the Union military hospital outside Richmond, Virginia. He had been shot through the body on the next to last day of the War Between the States, and between recuperating, and lying stunned and appalled at all he had seen for the previous two years, the conviction had come to James Carmichael that the only possible salvation for him, for all former Confederates and Yankees, in fact for all mankind, everywhere, lay through His Lord, Jesus Christ, and that was *James Carmichael's* salvation; that had been his escape, back in those years of horror when almost everything James Carmichael had believed very strongly in, including General Lee, President Jeff Davis, the total Confederate cause, had been swept away by a mighty and bloody mailed fist in a blue

Yankee uniform.

But that had been many years ago. During the interegnum, James Carmichael had aged, mellowed, broadened in the depth and scope of his intelligence, so when another wounded man from another war came to Reverend Carmichael thirty years later, seeking ordination in the church, Reverend Carmichael did not discourage him, in fact he prayed right beside him, even helped him study for the Ministry, and for a solid year worked at winnowing out the solid sense of horror and revulsion, then, when the younger man finally looked out at his world from wiser eyes, James Carmichael recognised the expression, and said, "Well, Phil, goodbye and good luck."

They had stood looking at one another for a bit, then Reverend Carmichael's eyes twinkled. Phil Gunhill's smile had come slowly, as it always did. Then they had laughed, had shaken hands, and Phil Gunhill rode out of the Sioux Mission at Fallen Timber, Montana Territory, with James Carmichael's soundless prayers.

They would never meet again.

Spring followed winter, summer followed springtime, the sky kept getting bluer, the land greener, the creek-water kept tasting colder and better as the heat of the land increased, and as long as a man did not stray much below the high escarpment that prevented Colorado from slipping down into New Mexico, which was desert country; at least in summertime it was *arid* country, he would not run out of greenery and snow-water creeks, and forest-shade.

Gunhill crossed down out of Montana and spent an entire long springtime and early summer exploring Wyoming, a rugged, largely mountainous land where the wind blew cold on the high plains until almost August. The day he walked his horse over the boundary line into Colorado, at a squalid village called Tie Siding, because that was where the railroad's builders had stacked their roadbed wooden ties, the wind kept pushing from behind as though it were, in fact, Gunhill's destiny and it was urging him onward. Maybe it was.

The land turned warm by the time he was well southward. Otherwise, it changed only very gradually, becoming a little less rugged and sere, becoming richer where the ground-depth ran deeper, enabling more diverse forms of growth to flourish. What had been plains and prairie upon the Montana and Wyoming plateaux were called 'parks' in Colorado, and while they looked similar, they were different because of that deeper, blacker, rich soil.

Gunhill did not stay on the stageroad which ran southward from Laramie to Tie Siding, down to Virginia Dale, and through the rugged uplands out to the Fort Collins country, he turned off and passed through the solitude of cathedral forests, down across the green parks, camped beside trout streams, crested rolling low hills, skirted cattle ranges, bypassed an occasional set of sturdy log ranch buildings, and once he sat in filagreed tree shade watching a straggling band of Hadatsas making a noisy, dusty trail of unshod hooves, travois skid-marks, as the Indians went in search of a hunting ground, dogs running among the horses, old crones flailing left and right with sticks and shrieking imprecations at raffish, snake-eyed children who would not stay near the family place in the slovenly line of march, and watched as bare-chested youths herded along a band of half-broke horses, also shouting and brandishing quirts.

He knew the Hidatsas. Other Sioux called them "Big Bellies" because of their habit of dropping in, an entire clan of them, to visit their relatives, and eating everything in sight until, locust-like, they packed up and went straggling off again. Those visits frequently lasted for months.

Gunhill had sat and watched, and had smiled to himself, wondering what hard-working, unsuspecting branch of the Dakota Nation those Big Bellies were going to descend upon, this time. Then, when the Indians were gone, he continued on down the far side of his low hill and told his horse that people were pretty much the same, in the essentials.

That same afternoon his horse cast a shoe, which would not have been a cause for worry if Gunhill had been travelling a country where sharp rock didn't predominate. But even so, the hoof would probably not wear down to the quick for another day or so. Then, of course, the horse would get 'ouchy' and begin to flinch every time he touched down over jagged rock.

That night Gunhill made his camp in a bosque of unkempt old bull-pines near a narrow, hurrying little white-water creek, and the following morning he rode out of the trees into an emerald world of rich, dark green meadows that stretched, necklace-like, for miles, and had narrow belts of pines and fir trees separating each 'park' from the adjoining 'park'.

Except for one thing, all that miles-deep expanse of primeval uplands seemed as empty as it had been for perhaps ten thousand years. The exception were little bunches of fat cattle, their red hides shiny with health, their calves sassy and bright-eyed, with broad backs and double chins. The youngest critters showed the brand best; they hadn't been wearing it very long. From a distance Gunhill took it to be a tent, or a pitched-roof tipi, but when an occasional little stiff-standing critter, consumed with curiosity, stood until the very last moment, Gunhill saw that the brand was not a tipi, it was an arrow. The two slanting high lines were symbolic of the silhouetted sides of an arrowhead, but from mid-way up there was a third line, straight down, and that signified the arrow-shaft. It was a neat, uncluttered mark, easy to read and easy to burn on. In fact a man running that mark on a greasy red rib-cage didn't actually need an orthodox iron at all, all he needed was a straight-bar iron, or a running iron. It seemed to Gunhill as he passed those little bunches of grazing cattle, that the running iron *had* been used; the brands varied in size, which they couldn't have done, on freshly marked animals, if a stamp-iron had been used.

Those were bred-up, quality cattle, too. The cows were broad-backed, deep-bellied, large critters. The calves were already half as large as most yearlings, and they were still sucking. Breeding-up had only been the livestockman's fetish for about ten or fifteen years; most of the big outfits still ran thousands of head of cattle showing the earlier, Texas bloodlines; those longhorn-crosses were tougher, more resourceful, than the bred-up redbacks Gunhill was passing among, but the day had just about passed when cattle had to compete with bears and cougars and buffalo and wolves on the open range; they no longer needed a six-foot spread of horns nor the nasty temperament of Longhorns, to survive.

Gunhill saw the buildings, finally, quite by accident. He had decided to avoid people, any and all kinds of people, when he had last shaken hands with Reverend James Carmichael, and up until now he had managed it well enough, but there was a pressing circumstance that kept him sitting on a sidehill studying the ranch buildings he'd inadvertently stumbled upon, which he could not postpone much longer. He was riding a three-legged horse.

He did not know where he was nor whether there might be a town somewhere close by. He could not put off nailing a new shoe on his animal much longer. If he bypassed this cow outfit as he'd been doing for months now when he saw buildings, he could very easily end up leading, not riding, a lame horse.

He had decided to ride on down, buy a shoe, borrow someone's forge and anvil for an hour or so, then head on out again, and was in fact lifting his reinhand, to push down across the great green meadow, when someone behind him in the trees came clattering down from higher up calling ahead.

"Hey, Jasper, you're not supposed to be up here."

Gunhill twisted for an uphill look. The rider was young, with taffy hair, a battered grey floppy old hat, and was wearing a faded blue workshirt that had been scrubbed but not ironed. The boots were scuffed, the spurs were California style, silver mounted to match the half-breed bit, and the horse was a chestnut gelding, sleek as burnished copper. It was the horse that really held Gunhill's attention as the rider angled back and forth through the long descent. That the rider had mistaken Gunhill for someone else was obvious, and of no particular concern.

When the rider got close enough and raised dark blue eyes to speak again, Gunhill got a shock. It wasn't a *man,* it was a *girl.*

She said, "I didn't find anything except an

old wolf lair." Then she stopped speaking and stared. "You're not Jasper."

Gunhill could agree with that, and if someone had named him Jasper, he wasn't so sure he'd have kept that name, either.

The girl reined up, her tanned, perfect features gradually hardening. "Who are you and what are you doing sitting up here like an Indian, spying on the ranch?"

Gunhill did not answer right away. She couldn't have been over perhaps eighteen or twenty; she was lithe but rounded, the golden-taffy hair tucked under the floppy old battered Stetson hat glinted with light and dark brilliance even in this forested place where sunlight barely reached. She was beautiful — or else Gunhill had been by himself too long.

"I asked who you were?" she exclaimed.

Gunhill's answer was calm, almost laconic. "Just riding through. My name's Phil Gunhill. I'm from Montana, originally." He pointed. "My horse cast a shoe yesterday afternoon. I was just sitting here wondering, if I rode down to those buildings yonder, would the folks there sell me a shoe and let me use their fire and anvil to nail it on."

The violet eyes sought out that bare hoof before very deliberately and systematically lifting to examine Gunhill, his horse, his saddle, his light pack behind the cantle, his booted Winchester, and finally the tied-down, ivory-stocked Colt on his left hip. The girl considered this gun longest, and when she ultimately looked Gunhill in the face, she said, "You're left-handed?"

Gunhill felt like smiling at her inquisitiveness, instead he simply nodded. "Now, if you're from down there at those buildings, and if you've finished your inspection, maybe you'd tell me — will they sell me a shoe and let me use their shop to put it on?"

The girl did not take her eyes off Gunhill's face as she slowly bobbed her head. "They won't *sell* you a shoe, but you're welcome to take one and nail it on. Come along . . . What did you say your name was?"

"Gunhill. Phil Gunhill."

They started down towards the meadow side by side.

2

The buildings were not old, but there was no bark peeling nor sap running, either, so Gunhill guessed they might have been erected perhaps eight or ten years earlier. The log barn was massive; it stood as an obvious monument to someone's pride, not only in his accomplishment of erecting it, but in his pride in his land and cattle — and in himself.

There were smaller sheds of the kind every ranch-yard had, a bunkhouse, forge-shop, buggy and wagon shed, a massive-walled smokehouse, even a log chicken-house with a slat-fence runway.

As Gunhill rode closer, saying nothing and unaware that he was under a close, sidelong scrutiny, the impression he got was of thrift, resourcefulness, unstinting enterprise, all the things a man had to possess to successfully pioneer in the far places, and perhaps most of all, an impression of a man's pride in himself and what he could accomplish with his mind and his hands.

The girl suddenly said, “Do you approve, Mr Gunhill?”

He turned, looked at the lovely face beneath the threadbare and battered old wide-brimmed rider’s hat, suppressed a smile and nodded. “I approve. It’s a beautiful setting — mountains back a ways, timber, emerald meadows. And there’s a man down there who knows his mind.”

She turned away and said nothing more until they entered the yard, then she pointed. “That’s the shoeing shed. Help yourself to whatever you need.”

As they swung off out front of the barn at the tie-rack, she glanced towards the log bunkhouse. There was a man sitting out there in a home-made chair, with a massive white-bandaged leg propped in front of him, with his black hat tilted back, eyeing them from porch-shadows. The girl said, “That’s who I thought you were.”

Gunhill looked. “That’s why you said I wasn’t supposed to be up there — that broken leg?”

“Yes. That’s Jasper. He’s not supposed to climb onto a horse for an other couple of weeks. From the back I thought . . . Well; there aren’t very many other people out here, Mr Gunhill."

"One thing you forgot," said Gunhill, and at the girl's look of enquiry, Gunhill smiled slowly. "You didn't tell me your name."

"Gloryann. Gloryann Spencer." She turned to lead her horse into the barn and Gunhill, who had only seen her on a horse, lingered at the tie-rack, watching her walk away.

He sighed, lugged off his outfit, shed his jacket and took the chunky, short-backed, slant-eyed bay horse across the yard to the shoeing shed.

It was hot, once he fired up the forge. Even though the shed, like most ranch-yard shoeing sheds, only had three sides, was entirely open in front, the roof was low, and today the sun was almost directly overhead, to help bring the interior temperature up to where Gunhill's shirt turned steadily darker, in streaks, as he worked.

He did not see the girl again, nor did he particularly look for her. Otherwise, the yard was unusually quiet. A ranch this size ordinarily had at least a couple of riders close by. There was usually some noise, even if it was only restless horses in a corral, or perhaps a bull penned up for doctoring.

Gunhill pared down, tested the shoe, beat it curved, flattened it, dowelled out the holes atop the anvil, and tried it again. The second time the fit was perfect. A hard voice from the yard in front said, "I never get 'em right until the third or fourth fit."

Gunhill looked up. The man was about Gunhill's age and about his size, but he was swarthy, black-eyed and black-haired, to Gunhill's fairer shades. He walked with the aid of a whittled-on stick. His right leg had been splinted and bound round and round until it looked twice as thick as his other leg. Gunhill said, "You don't look like you'll be doing any shoeing for a while yet."

The black-eyed man limped in, eased down upon a horseshoe keg, sighed and placed the stick across his knees. "I won't," he said. "Ann said she found you up a side-hill on the north meadow."

Gunhill stooped, hoisted the horse's bare foot and reached for two nails and the farrier's hammer. "Yep. She came down from higher up all set to bawl me out because she thought I was you. Called me Jasper."

The black-eyed man watched Gunhill tap in the first nail and get set to drive in the second one. "Yeah, she told me." He suddenly grinned, showing white, perfect large teeth. "Good thing it wasn't me. She'd have raised hell and propped it up."

Gunhill worked in silence until he had all

the nails driven and clinched, then he reached for the nail-set, and paused to look over where the black-eyed man was sitting. "Cattle sure look good," he said. "Slick as moles. I saw some calves looked like they'd only been marked a short while back."

"Two weeks, thereabouts," said the black-eyed man. "That's when I busted this thing. Roped a calf on foot, the little devil didn't run *away* from me the way they always do, it run right between my legs, and it was bawling bloody murder, so the old cow was charging. Gloryann couldn't cut the cow back. I was up in the air from the rope, when the old cow caught me coming down. Then she trampled on the leg, busting it."

"Why didn't one of the other riders drag her off?" asked Gunhill, completing the clinches and reaching for the rasp, still bent with the hoof between his knees.

"What other riders? Gloryann's the only other rider besides me. Her mother don't ride."

Gunhill rasped hard until the job was finished, let the hoof down and straightened up. He gazed with frank curiosity at the black-eyed cowboy. "Just you and the girl? Just the two of you did all the marking and what-not? Mister, I rode through what I figure must have been several hundred cows with calves."

"Closer to four hundred cows," said the injured man. "Sure, Ann and I done it. We strung it out over a month, and lucky for us, I didn't get hurt until the last damned day."

Gunhill began to thoughtfully put the tools exactly where he had found them. When he was finished, he went to a hanging earthen jar and drank deeply of the cold water, then he kicked up another shoe-keg, sank down upon it and started rolling a cigarette as he said, "Jasper, that's not a very big crew for handling four hundred cows."

The black-eyed man nodded wryly. "No, it isn't." He leaned, sighted on something, and raised his walking stick as though he were aiming a rifle. "See that cleared place south of the main-house atop the little hill?"

"Yes."

"Well; that's where Harold Spencer is buried." Jasper straightened on the keg and leaned a little when he pushed his stick into the ground. "He died four months back. That left Gloryann and her maw. And me. There was two other riders in the springtime, but when Mr Spencer died they drew their time and rode on."

Gunhill turned this over in his mind, and understood the girl's strained look and sudden silence when they'd been approaching the barn, and Gunhill had said something about the man who'd developed this place being a person who knew his mind. He inhaled, exhaled, pushed sweat off his forehead with a limp sleeve, and looked at Jasper from beneath dark, arched brows.

"The other two riders — they wouldn't work for a woman?"

Jasper closed both hands atop his walking stick and rested his chin upon them. "Nope. Would you?"

Gunhill knew the range prejudices as well as any man; he'd drawn top pay a time or two in his lifetime. He did not answer. "It hasn't killed you, has it, Jasper?"

The black eyes kindled ironically. "Well; not quite."

They both laughed and Gunhill dropped his smoke, stamped it out and returned to the water-jug for another long drink.

The big, husky cowboy with the splinted leg arose, hitched around to look yonder across the empty, golden-lighted yard, and as Gunhill followed out Jasper's line of sight, he saw the girl, only now she was hatless. Her hair was short-cropped, curly, and when she walked it changed from gold to copper then back to gold again. She had a purposeful stride. Gunhill's slow smile came.

"She acts like a boss," he murmured, then turned to take his gunbelt off a peg and swing it round his middle.

Jasper eyed the ivory handled gun as though he might comment on it, then he said, "Where you headed, Mr Gunhill? West from here there's a town about thirty miles. It's called Crow's Landing. It's on the far side of the Crow River. Otherwise, you'll be travelling through mountains. You might see some In'ian camps, but that's about all you'll see."

Gunhill, remembering the Hidatsas, told Jasper of that interlude, with a comment about some luckless tribesmen about to be descended upon, and Jasper laughed. "You know 'em," he said, eyeing Gunhill a little more closely. "You from Montana, by any chance?"

It wasn't a wide guess; Montana was Sioux country. Gunhill turned to lead his horse out of the shed, out of the breathless heat. "Yeah. My last stop was at Fallen Timber. My next stop — who knows?"

"Just riding?"

"Yup. Been at it since late winter." Gunhill was followed out where the air was a little cooler by the injured rider. He watered his slant-eyed bay horse, leaned on the beast's back, both arms hooked over, and studied the open meadow northward where cattle were distantly visible. "Jasper, you better hire on a couple more men. One more, anyway. I'm not saying the girl isn't handy ahorseback and maybe even with a rope, but it's not the same."

The black-eyed man sighed. "Amen, it's not the same. You ever bust a leg?"

"Nope."

"Well, it hurts like hell, and there I was lying, waiting for that old cow to give up and take her lousy calf off into the timber, and I couldn't say a word. That was the worst part, Mr Gunhill. I couldn't say a single damned word because the only ones that come into my mind was the kind you dasn't say in front of womenfolk. I liked to strangled on my own tongue. So — you're absolutely right, it's not the same. But, as for hiring riders — I can't ride over to Crow's Landing. I can't even straddle a horse for another week or two. I'm sure not going to send *her* over there; it's a rough little town. So I'll get along as best I can until I'm able to make the trip."

Gunhill pondered Jasper's predicament a moment, then offered a suggestion. "If you'd like, I can head over that way and maybe send you back a couple of men. But it's a little late in the season to be hiring on; I'd guess most good men are already signed up."

The black-eyed leaned on his stick studying Gunhill. "How about you?" he asked. "I need at least one good man right now, not next month."

Gunhill's answer was a rueful head-shake. "You've got the marking done. They looked pretty well calved-out to me, and there shouldn't be much to do now for a few months but ride, keeping track of them. You can get along with the girl."

He led his horse across to the wide barn-opening where he'd dumped his saddle, and bent to shake out the blanket before pitching it across the bay horse's back. Jasper hitched over, following after, and studied Gunhill's outfit with an experienced eye.

He said, "The grub is the best you'll ever eat, and like you say, the work's not going to be hard for a while again. And Mrs Spencer'll pay you decent wages. There'd only be the two of us in the bunkhouse — plenty of room, Mr Gunhill."

From over in the hen-run a great commotion started up. The girl was over there gathering eggs. As Gunhill hoisted the saddle to ease it down upon his horse's back, he saw that coppery-gold head bob in and out as the girl went from nest to nest. "*Two* lady bosses," he murmured, more to the bay horse than to the man standing against the barn.

Jasper heard, and commented. "You have to set down a little on the girl, now and then, but her mother's the finest lady I ever knew. Mr Spencer was like that. That's why I'm still here. I told him I'd stay when he got sick. But I sure never figured he'd die. Anyway, a man gives his word, he stands by it."

Gunhill finished cinching up, turned, hat on the back of his head, fished out a silver cartwheel and flipped it. As Jasper instinctively raised a hand to catch the coin, Gunhill said, "I'm obliged for the shoe and the use of the tools." He saw the black eyes come up, read what lay in their depths and shook his head. "I don't take charity, Jasper. My horse and I pay our way. I'm right obliged to you folks." He turned the horse, stepped over leather, smiled, and rode out of the yard.

3

Those emerald meadows ran across the westerly country for miles, each one separated from the others by stands of timber. To the north were high mountains, distant enough so that they seemed to almost blend in a blur of hazy blue with the slatey skies. Straight ahead, in the direction Gunhill was riding, there were more mountains, but not as distant nor as high and craggy. They had forested slopes. Gunhill had been crossing that kind of high country since he'd left Fallen Timber. The other kind, that northerly cordillera, was the kind of country a man avoided at all costs if he could. Not just because those were real mountains and reached more than a mile straight up, but because they were walls of granite and had precious little horse feed in them.

Gunhill nooned in a shady place, off-saddled to allow the chunky bay horse to fill up, and lay back watching cloud-shapes, an occupation any man who had ever drifted much, alone, through the uninhabited upland world, got in the habit of doing while he loafed. Sometimes, a drifter did the same thing in his blankets when total night was down, studied the overhead world and tried a little — not too hard — to figure out what it was all about. You never found any real startling answers, but you sure eventually came to understand one thing; about the least significant ambulatory critter in the Universe was the drifter coursing indifferently across the whole curve of a continent.

Gunhill thought of Jasper. Part Indian; maybe Sioux, maybe Crow or Cheyenne. Anyway, he was too big and strong to be part Southwestern redskin. Likeable, sensible, even-tempered-seeming man.

He also thought of Gloryann, while he was lying back watching the cloud shapes assume a formation of flying great galleons, all sails full. She was lithe and strong and golden, and looked a man squarely in the eyes when she talked. Gunhill sat up, sighed, rolled a smoke and shook his head thinking how odd it was that a girl with whom he had only exchanged maybe a dozen sentences, would remain exactly as she now was, forever, in his mind. When he was an old man, even, he would remember her exactly as he had first seen her. Everything else would change in Gunhill's lifetime — but that memory. Perhaps the oddest part was his knowing that this would be so.

A big bull elk came shambling down out of some northward trees, paused when the bay horse moved, stood like an oil painting for a long time, sniffing and looking, then, having decided it was only a solitary horse, stepped out onto the meadow and began a long crossing towards the forest to the south, which was about a mile distant, but which, in the glass-clear air, seemed only a hundred yards off. Gunhill smoked, watched, and admired the powerful big animal.

Later, when he saw his horse stop grazing and turn his back to the sunlight, full as a tick and ready to drowse, Gunhill arose to go catch the animal. There was rusty-red movement to his left, around the tree-tier from him. He stopped dead-still and looked. Several wet cows came along, baby calves at their sides, grazing their way into this green park. Gunhill walked on down, caught the horse, led it back and rigged it out. At first, the cows were wary and high-headed, which was normal; they had baby calves with them, but when Gunhill barely more than glanced in their direction, they decided he was no threat and resumed grazing.

Gunhill stepped astride, pointed his horse towards the retreating hills, and allowed the bay to pick both their route and their gait.

The sun was slanting off-centre, the heat was softened by a pale haze, there were birds in almost every tree Gunhill passed who scolded him for intruding, and when he was almost completely across the big meadow, he saw a solitary young Hereford critter standing in speckled tree-shade, head up, eyes wide, watching him with a very intent stare. He knew the look and he surmised the problem behind it, but before he had a chance to angle wide to relieve the animal's great anxiety, a rider charged through from the southward trees, rope down, big loop built, and because the cow was so intently watching the horsemen in front of her, she did not even hear the roper until it was almost too late. Then she whirled, snorting like a Texas steer, and after one look, hoisted her tail and fled. But she was not in shape for running. The rope sailed high, settled a yard ahead, the heifer shoved her head into the loop, and the rider set up the horse.

Gunhill paused to watch. When the cow, a good thousand-pounder, hit the end of that lariat, she was swung violently around. She lost her footing in the grass, but the rider's horse, perhaps not expecting so much weight, perhaps just not that savvy a rope-horse, was not braced. He went down head-first, jerked all the way to his knees. The rider sailed overhead and landed hard, fifty feet beyond the horse.

Gunhill had seen a jerk-down before. He spun and made a run to get between the downed rider and the wild-eyed young cow. He made it only because the critter was having trouble regaining its feet. He glanced, and thought the cow might have broken a leg. It was floundering, blowing spittle, rolling its eyes, and falling back down after each fight to get upright.

Gunhill reached the shaken horse, standing wide-legged and half-stunned, in time to talk it back down to a relatively calm state, then he walked out where the rider was beginning to stir.

It was Gloryann Spencer. The last he had seen of her, she'd been gathering eggs at the ranch-yard. He was astonished, but he was also in a poor position to start a conversation, if that cow ever got upright, so he stopped caught her by the shoulders, lifted her to her feet and held her at arm's length.

"You hurt?" he asked.

She did not lift her face to him, but she shook her head. "No. It's the heifer that needs help."

Gunhill looked — and got his second surprise. The critter hadn't broken a leg, she had come to her time, but the calf was hung up. One small, yellowish, soft hoof showed. The cow was beating the ground with her head and lying in a bowed position as she strained. Gloryann was right, the heifer could not calve without help. Gunhill had pulled his share of hung-up calves. He left the girl standing loosely, head-hung and none too steady, took down his lariat, circled round the profusely sweating heifer, saw the un-focusing eyes, the lolling tongue, knew it was safe to get in closer, and went round behind. He didn't have time to shed his jacket and shirt nor even to roll up his sleeve. He hunkered back there and went instantly to work. When he had the little critter aimed right, forelegs protruding, head down over the legs, he secured the lariat, walked back, waited until the cow convulsed, then leaned. He had to do this four times, then the calf slid out, wet and membrane-encased.

With an eye on the cow, Gunhill went forward and with one hand tore the membrane around the calf's nostrils, with the other hand retrieved his lariat, then he wasted no time getting away from there. The cow, though, had evidently been all night in labour; she couldn't have jumped up and charged Gunhill if she'd thought of it, and right now she was just lying there panting, eyes closed, her entire body rising and falling as she sucked in great gulps of air.

Gloryann was down again, over beside her horse. The horse, in fact, seemed to be the least concerned of them all. Except for grass stains across his chest and shoulder, he looked fine.

Gunhill coiled the rope, draped it from his saddlehorn, pushed back his hat and squatted beside the girl.

She did not look at him this time, either, as she said, "I think it's my ankle. I think I broke it when I fell." Then, finally, she raised her cornflower-blue eyes. "Will you help me into the saddle?"

He nodded, but did not stand up. He studied her horse, looked over where the cow was stirring, finally, raising up to anxiously eye the bundle of feebly threshing new life behind her. Then he said, "You ever rope off that horse before?"

She shook her head. "No, and I didn't expect to have to this time either. I was just checking the drift. Most of our animals are all calved out. I saw her, off by herself, and went to look."

Gunhill nodded. He knew the rest of it. In a gently chiding tone he said, "Annie, the next time, don't even try it on a green horse unless you're close enough to some trees to head around them and hold the cow before she breaks your neck — or your horse's neck."

The blue eyes came up. "I didn't do that on purpose, Mr Gunhill."

He did not relent. "That wouldn't make a bit of difference if you'd broken your back in that fall. You're miles from the ranch. You'd lie out here until you died." He pondered all this for a moment, then, in a different tone, asked a question. "How did you get out here, anyway; the last I saw, you were gathering eggs in the hen-run."

"I rode out a few minutes after you did," she answered, avoiding his stare again. "Will you help me into the saddle now — if you've finished the scolding."

He stood up, took her by the arms and lifted. She came up the front of him, balancing on one leg, and although she looked tall, because she was long-legged and lithe, when he looked down, her face was almost six inches lower than his chin.

She leaned and clung to him, then twisted

to look over where her horse stood. "If you'll hold my hand, I'll hop over and —"

He bent, scooped her up in both arms and walked to the horse, boosted her gently into the saddle, and when she winced he said, "You're not going to be much good to Jasper now, for a while."

She had the reins in her left hand and was holding her side with the right hand. In a slightly breathless gasp she said, "My side. My ribs too."

Gunhill lowered his arms, once she was up there. "What do you mean, your ribs? You landed on your *back.*"

She gingerly massaged her side. "Right here. It hurts when I breathe and when I try to sit straight." She put a darkening gaze downward. "I know I landed on my back, but here is where it hurts. Here, and my left ankle."

Gunhill considered for a moment, then went round to his own horse, stepped up, strapped the lariat into place at the swells, and rode over to take the reins from her and turn back in the direction of the ranch. She held to the saddlehorn with her left hand. Once, she twisted to see where the cow was; the critter was back there, close to the trees, washing her newborn calf and nuzzling it.

Gunhill was not exactly pleased at having to ride all the way back to the Arrow Ranch, but he wasn't actually very annoyed either; he did not have a destination, actually, so if he lost a day it wasn't going to inconvenience him. But he *was* a little disgusted. When they had been moving about an hour, he let her mount come up abreast of him.

"If you're going to rope, you'd better understand that there's more to it than just charging like a bloody-hand buck and swinging your rope. In time, anyone can learn to catch a critter, but that's just the beginning."

Her violet eyes swung, blazing, but she checked whatever had been on the tip of her tongue, and looked swiftly away. For a hundred yards she was silent, but at the end of that distance she said, "I didn't have time to go back to the ranch for my rope horse, Mr Gunhill. That heifer would have hidden in the trees, and she'd have died."

That was true enough. Gunhill gave up, re-settled his hat, eyed the distance, studied landmarks, knew about where he was and when they would reach the yard, and didn't say another word. But he *thought* a few: Poor Jasper, having to rely on this headstrong, boy-built, courageously idiotic and inexperienced *female* girl.

Well; damned few men in this life ever seemed to be able to master their own destiny, and evidently Jasper was, like Phil Gunhill, one of those luckless fellers.

He made a smoke, slouched in the late-day pleasant warmth, led her along like a Brulé warrior with a captive-squaw, and indifferently wondered how anyone who had landed on their *back,* straight out, could have broken or cracked some ribs.

4

On Gunhill's previous brief visit to Arrow, he had not met Gloryann's mother, but this time he met her when he unloaded her daughter out front of the main-house and helped the girl up the steps to the veranda. The older woman was startlingly like her daughter. Slightly thicker and there was a handsome shade of grey over each ear, but otherwise their features were alike, and their colouring. Mrs Spencer was too distraught over her daughter's injured condition to be more than perfunctorily polite, so Gunhill was unable to form much of an opinion of the older woman. She swept a strong arm round Gloryann's waist and helped her into the house.

Gunhill took the girl's horse, and his own animal, down to the barn, left his horse at the tie-rack out front, entered the barn's shadowy, cool interior with the other animal and went to work off-saddling and offbridling.

The horse was beginning to stiffen a little. When he had the beast stripped, Gunhill walked him the length of the barn, then abruptly turned back. As the horse tried to turn close, he faltered, which was what Gunhill had expected and was watching for.

From the front entranceway a man's voice said, "Jammed in the shoulders. What happened?"

Gunhill led the horse forward, closer to where Jasper was supporting himself with his walking stick, and explained. "The girl roped a calvy heifer. She got jerked down. I took her to the house. She's got hurt ribs and a sore ankle. The horse'll be all right in a few days — providing you don't confine him in a stall, where he'll stock up and get stiff as a post."

Jasper nodded. "I'll turn him out in a corral." Jasper gazed at Gunhill. "You happened along?"

"No. *She* happened along. I'd been nooning and was just riding off when she busted out of the trees after the heifer." Gunhill looked over at Jasper. "I suppose you could say it was just one of those things — except that I think a *man* would have ridden his roping horse, because he would have wanted to be prepared for anything he encountered.

But maybe I'm being hard on the girl."

Jasper said, "Yeah, maybe," dryly, and would have hobbled over to take the lead-rope and turn the horse into an outside corral, but Gunhill did not relinquish the rope. He took the horse out back and turned him into a round-corral, then leaned on the stringers back there, watching as the horse walked in a diminishing circle until he found just the right spot, where the dust was softest, and lay down to roll, first onto one side, then onto the other side.

Jasper limped up, tilted back his hat, watched the horse a moment, then smiled. "Worth a hunnert dollars for each time he can roll completely over."

Gunhill had heard this old adage, and smiled back. "Two hundred dollars worth of horse, but I'll tell you one thing, Jasper, he won't weigh over nine hundred and fifty pounds, and almost any cow full of calf will weigh better'n a thousand — so if a person's going to be roping big cows, he'd sure better use a horse they can't jerk down." Gunhill turned. "Seems to me you people've had your share of bad luck lately."

Jasper continued to lean, staring at the horse. "You know half of it; Mr Spencer died, I broke a leg, now my helper's hurt too."

"What's the other half?"

"Remember when she found you, and the way she acted?"

"Yes."

"Well; we lost fifty head of steers a week ago. She was trying to track them." Jasper put his black gaze on Gunhill. "You know how steers are; they got no reason to stay, especially this time of year when there's feed and water just about anywhere they want to wander."

That was true enough; castration altered more than just the physical aptitudes of bull calves. A steer never developed much of a homing instinct, after he'd been cut, which was why, when the feed was good and every creek had water in it, cow outfits kept their riders on the range turning back drifters.

Gunhill gazed in quiet thought at the swarthy man. "No trace of them?"

"Nope. They're just plain gone," replied Jasper. "She's no good at tracking; what woman is? This time of year with all the cattle scattered, it takes a pretty damned savvy rider to be able to tell one kind of track from the other. You know about that?"

Gunhill knew. "Yeah. But when I was passing inland I didn't see many cattle until I reached your Arrow range. They shouldn't be all that hard to find."

Jasper turned, settling his back against the peeled-log corral stringers with the sun against his shoulders. His glance ranged over a lot of country. "Sitting in a rocking chair on a bunkhouse porch, Mr Gunhill, a man don't get over a lot of country, does he?"

Gunhill could almost *hear* what Jasper was thinking. He sighed to himself, cast a final glance at the horse, then he too turned and leaned back. He did not want a job; he did not want any responsibility nor did he want to feel under any obligations.

Jasper said, "The ranch won't go under over the loss of fifty steers. Miz' Spencer'll still be here next year and maybe the year after. But that kind of a loss hurts, and Arrow isn't one of those five-thousand-head cow outfits. If her husband had lived, in time he might have bred up to maybe two or three times what the land is carrying now; he kept back all his good heifers. But he's dead. And like you said — bad luck seems to come in bunches. One thing is a gut-cinch, though; no woman can keep a cow outfit by herself." Jasper fished for his tobacco sack and rolled a brown-paper smoke. After lighting up, and still without looking at Gunhill, he concluded his musing. "The handwritin' on the wall is over there against those northward mountains. I don't think I want to be around here when everything caves in. I've been sitting on that damned porch yonder, figuring that what I'll do when I'm able, is pull out, heading north."

Gunhill knew what personal defeat tasted like; it was bitter as gall. It was demoralising, and it made a man lose the two things no man could do much without: hope, and some kind of goal.

Without much enthusiasm, but without sounding resentful, he said, "I'll hang around for a couple of weeks, Jasper. Until you're able to ride again." As the black-eyes swung around, Gunhill smiled crookedly. "You don't need a rider, really, except to find those steers. It shouldn't take long to do that."

That ended the conversation. Gunhill went out front where his horse was patiently standing, led him into the log barn again, for the second time in the same day, off-saddled him, cuffed him good, then put him into a stall and forked feed down from the loft. After that, he peeled his bedroll and saddlebags off and lugged them to the bunkhouse where Jasper had gone earlier.

Gunhill chose a lower bunk, near the door, unrolled his blankets, hung the booted

Winchester from a wooden peg nearby, settled his personal things out back at the wash-bench, where a steel shaving mirror hung, and when he returned Jasper had set out a bottle of whiskey and two glasses on the big table in the centre of the room. Without a word, Jasper poured both glasses full, shoved one across and eased down on the far side of the table with the other glass in his dark, scarred right hand.

Gunhill hung up his hat, slung his shell-belt and gun from the same peg, and sauntered to the table to sit down and reach for the whiskey. He wasn't much of a drinker; had never really developed much of a taste for the stuff. Not because he was hide-bound, but simply because he had grown up in a home where people had rarely drunk, and by the time he'd sampled his first few drinks, he'd been pretty well established in his taste and habits. Whiskey simply did not taste pleasant to Gunhill.

He said, "One of us had better tell Mrs Spencer I'm on the place."

Jasper agreed. "I'll do it. She'll be grateful."

Gunhill looked at the whiskey, then resolutely hoisted the glass as he said, "She won't owe me any gratitude. I never cared much for the word, Jasper." He downed the whiskey, shoved the glass away and rolled a cigarette under Jasper's black gaze. As he loosened and leaned comfortably upon the table, he said, "No dog, Jasper? Hell of a cow ranch that doesn't have at least one dog on it."

"There was one," stated the injured man. "Big, stout, good-natured one, in fact."

When that was all Jasper had to say, Gunhill guessed the rest of it. "He died."

"Yeah; but I don't figure that had anything to do with the run of bad luck. He was old. The Spencers brought him up from New Mexico with them."

"That's where they're from?"

"Yeah. Somewhere in the hill country behind Taos. They ranched down there, but it was brush-country without any rain at all some years, and never with very much. Mr Spencer rode through here one time taking cattle to Cheyenne. The very next year he sold out down there and come up here."

"How much land does Arrow own, and where are the lines?"

"West about five miles past where you helped Ann. East about the same distance. Southward, we go down to a big, black barranca where there's an old drover-trail, and northward, Mr Spencer was never sure where his line was, but we always figured it went about six or seven miles up across all the big meadows and fetched up along the base of some granite foothills."

Gunhill was surprised and showed it. "That's enough land to run five times as much livestock as you've got," he exclaimed, and Jasper nodded with a small, tough smile showing. "Yeah, I know. So did Mr Spencer. But he wouldn't borrow money to stock his range; he said he'd keep back his own stock and build up to his full capacity over the years. Now, I can see that he was right; his widow don't owe a cent to anyone, but when he and I used to ride together, I'd argue like hell that it was a waste of grass not to bring in more cattle." Jasper downed his whiskey and reached for the bottle. He let it hang above Gunhill's glass first. Gunhill shook his head, so Jasper re-filled only his own glass, then he stoppered the bottle and set it aside, hunched a little and said, "I believe a man'd ought to be honest with another man, Mr Gunhill." Jasper was gazing at the whiskey glass in his fist as he said this. "I'm talkin' about those fifty steers." He paused, turned the glass slowly in its little sticky puddle and did not raise his face. "Sittin' on that damned porch outside don't make me right, by a long sight, but I got an idea about those steers.

They went south, not north." The black eyes came up as Gunhill spoke.

"The girl was north when she came onto me. She was looking for them up —"

"I know," stated Jasper, "I sent her up in that direction."

Gunhill, returning Jasper's look, began to have a hunch. But he said nothing.

"What could she do if she found them, Mr Gunhill?"

"Drive them home — if she could."

"Yeah, and that's exactly it. *If she could.* You remember me telling you about those two riders who used to work on the ranch, who quit right after Mr Spencer died?"

"Yes."

"They went south; they told me the night before they pulled out they thought they'd go down on the desert for the rest of this year and maybe trap wild horses."

Gunhill blew out a big breath. "*They* went south, and you think the cattle also went south."

Jasper solemnly nodded. "Care for another drink, now?" he asked.

Gunhill still declined, so Jasper raised his own glass, drank it empty, and this time when he set it down, he shoved it beyond reach. "You understand why I told you I figure a man'd ought to be honest with another man? Mr Gunhill, I'm going to get those cattle back for Miz' Spencer, as soon as I can ride. I don't expect you to get into this this at all, but I figure you'd ought to know about it. All you got to do is sort of keep an eye on things for a couple more weeks. Forget about trying to track those cattle. Just mind the drift, pull a calf if you have to, keep the cows out of the trees where the wolves and bears and panthers'll pull them down. That's all." Jasper smiled. "And one more thing — do I have to call you *Mr* Gunhill for the next half a month?"

Gunhill laughed. "Nope. Phil will do just fine."

5

Gunhill and Jasper played black-jack that night after supper, and quietly discussed the two women up at the main-house. Gunhill's second meeting with Mrs Spencer was very different from his first meeting. He got the impression, as he and Jasper trooped into the main-house kitchen for supper, that Gloryann had made Gunhill heroic in the re-telling of her exciting interlude, and injury, on the west range.

It was a little embarrassing, so Gunhill ate his supper, mostly in silence, then got out of there and went down to the barn to look in on his horse, then to stand a moment in the pleasant twilight, thinking.

By the time he and Jasper sat down to the traditional after-supper card game, with coffee on the bunkhouse wood-stove, with the coal-oil lamp bringing brightness to the entire log room, except in its farthest corners, Gunhill's mood was mellow and reflective. He won at their card game, not much, and he was as indifferent a winner as he was a loser, and as Jasper spoke, Gunhill listened. Eventually, when he has a fair amount of background detail about the widow and her lithe daughter over at the main-house, he brought up the roundabout countryside, which Jasper knew and which Gunhill had never even seen, beyond some of the westerly range where he had been riding through, when Gloryann came bursting into his life like a bombshell.

It was a pleasant, predictable evening in the bunkhouse. The only thing that made it different from all evenings in all bunkhouses, was that instead of there being from six to twelve men, there were only Gunhill and Jasper.

By the time Gunhill and Jasper were ready to turn in, their understanding of one another had deepened without either one of them revealing more than the bare minimum about himself. Men, especially rangemen, could gauge and plumb and appraise another man's beliefs, sentiments, degrees of honour and truthfulness, temperament and disposition, without a lot of time wasted. Jasper never mentioned his antecedents, his background, or even his last name, but when Gunhill turned in that night, he knew the black-eyed man as well as he probably ever would, in all the ways that really mattered.

Jasper probably felt the same way, but there was one thing Jasper hadn't guessed; Gunhill had no intention, now that he was drawing Arrow wages, to allow the matter of those fifty lost steers to lie in abeyance until Jasper was able to take the trail. Hell; by then every blessed one of them could be hanging in some town's butcher shop; in a couple of weeks a pair of savvy rangemen could drive fifty steers halfway to Kingdom Come, and sell them.

The following morning, when Gunhill rode out, he was astride an Arrow horse, a big, ugly *grulla* gelding that looked as tough as whang and as long-lasting as eternity. Jasper was not around when Gunhill departed, or he might have wondered about something: Gunhill left the yard fully armed. Not just with his shellbelt and that ivory-butted Colt, but also with his Winchester slung under the fender. Rangeriders did not go armed unless they expected to pass through bear or cougar country. Normally, for just checking drift and getting acquainted with the land forms, they didn't bother packing weapons at all.

Gunhill rode northward only until he was

out of sight of the ranch, then he busted out the *grulla,* southward; tested the animal's power and endurance for a solid two hours, until he was thoroughly satisfied, then he hauled the big animal down to a walk, and when they came upon that old drover's trail Jasper had mentioned the night before, the *grulla* had his wind back and was warmed-out.

Gunhill was in a different variety of country from the upland emerald meadows. Down here, miles from the ranch, there was a miles-long escarpment of black stone like a fortress wall, separating the green and forested high-country from a more broken and savage land on southward.

The old drover's road — called that, but it was really nothing more than a wide trail — ran directly along at the base of the barranca. Gunhill wasted an hour finding a game-trail down off the bluffs to the trail. And almost at once he found sign that the trail had been used very recently, perhaps no more than a couple of days earlier. He poked along reading the sign. It took a few miles and a few more hours, but by the time he was eastward where the black-rock cliff-face began petering out, began dwindling downward until, in the near-distance, it became a series of broken low pinnacles overgrown with brush and trees and grass, he knew about as much as he would learn, and that was enough to interest him.

Cattle had been driven, not southward but eastward, over in the direction of that stageroad running down from the Laramie plains towards Fort Collins. There had been no more than fifty head in the drive, and exactly as Jasper had surmised, two riders had been doing the driving.

If those drovers had taken their cattle in almost any other direction, Gunhill would have been unable to surmise ahead; he was only familiar with the easterly country. That was the direction he had ridden from, to reach Arrow range.

Satisfied, finally, by early afternoon, he angled northwesterly up over the broken-rock country, abandoning the drover's road with its tell-tale tracks, and boosted the *grulla* over into a long-legged, loose lope until he was back up close to Arrow range, then he slacked off and went poking along looking for Arrow cattle until shortly before sundown.

He had covered about as many miles in this one long day as most men would have covered in a day and a half, and the ugly big *grulla* horse was still head-high when Gunhill drifted down into the yard and rode over in front of the barn to swing down and lead the horse inside.

He had the animal stripped and was currying him vigorously, when Jasper appeared in the late-day shadows up front, walking with his stick. Jasper seemed to suspect nothing. He hobbled down to a saddle-pole and eased his weight against the wall as he said, "Learn much about the lay of the range?"

Gunhill had indeed learned something. He replied laconically. "Covered enough ground to get some ideas; it's a big country."

"How'd the stock look?" asked Jasper, black eyes drifting to Gunhill's saddle — with its booted carbine.

"Fine; as many as I saw of them," Gunhill answered. "No reason for them not to look good. This country is a paradise for feed."

Jasper drifted his black gaze over the *grulla* horse. He studied the animal's hooves and fetlocks impassively as he said, "Yeah; it struck me that way first time I come through here. There's more feed in these parks up here than they've got in the whole damned territory of New Mexico. And they got water to-boot." The black eyes shifted a little, studying Gunhill. "Didn't have to pull any more calves?"

Gunhill smiled and continued vigorously

cuffing the horse. "No, and to be right honest with you, there's only one job I like less, and that's cleaning 'em out."

Jasper faintly smiled. "I understand. I got a weak stomach for that cleaning out too." He leaned and began making squiggly marks in the dust at his feet with the whittled-on walking stick. "Phil — you didn't ride the north range today," he said, softly.

Gunhill straightened up slowly and leaned to look across the *grulla's* back. "Did I tell you I rode the north range, Jasper?"

"No, but that's the direction you rode off this morning." The black eyes were dead level and steady. "Want me to tell you where you rode today?"

"Shoot."

"You rode south, down off the cliff to the old drover's trail."

Gunhill looked down at the dark man's bandaged leg. There was no sign of horsehair or horsesweat on the white wrappings. He looked up. "All right. What of it?"

Jasper pointed with his walking stick. "See that red clay dust on the *grulla's* fetlocks? You only find that colour dirt down below the black barranca." Jasper raised his face a little, as he pointed towards Gunhill's saddle. "You took along your Winchester."

Gunhill strode to the saddle-pole, pitched the curry comb and rice-bristle brush into the box over there, walked back to untie the horse and stall him before he decided how to answer. Then he said, "Jasper, you can't ride for two weeks. You know as well as I do that two weeks from now those fifty steers will be strung up on meat hooks somewhere, and tanners'll be turning their hides into saddle-leather." Gunhill put up the horse and turned, leaning on the stall door gazing back towards the black-eyed man. "You said something about folks being honest with one another. I'll be honest with you. As long as I'm shoving my boots under the Spencer supper table and sleeping under the Spencer bunkhouse roof, I watch out for Spencer interests. Any objections to that?"

Jasper had none. "Nope. No objections at all. Only you could damned well get killed, looking out too hard for the Spencer interests. One man, even if he's plumb right, isn't any match for *two* men. I can tell you from experience, those two rangeriders are big, tough, savvy cowboys. They might even have friends over at Crow's Landing."

"They didn't go west," stated Gunhill, "they went northeast, over in the direction of the Laramie-Fort Collins road."

Jasper cleared his throat, spat aside, lifted

his hat and re-settled it, then stood a moment pondering, his aquiline profile made darker than usual by the gathering late-day gloom inside the barn. Eventually he said, "How big a start have they got?"

"Couple days," Gunhill replied. "But on the way back I think maybe I came up with a way to cut that down to practically nothing. I came inland to this ranch on an angling southwesterly course. I know the country between here and the Laramie plains, northward of Virginia Dale up in the direction of Tie Siding, over the line into Wyoming. If they stay to the trail, and if I cut diagonally northeastward, we'd ought to meet somewhere up near the border; maybe a few miles over it into Wyoming . . . Jasper, they weren't pushing their drive."

The black-eyed man nodded. "No reason for them to push it, Phil. I'm laid up, Mr Spencer is dead, and they don't know about you; all they know is that Gloryann and her maw can ride a little; Gloryann can ride the most. Who'd be afraid of a long-legged, coppery-headed girl?"

"I'll be on the trail before sun-up in the morning," stated Gunhill. "I'll take that same big *grulla* horse. He's rangy and tough as a boiled owl."

Jasper leaned on his stick looking distressed. "Gawddammit; maybe, if I slung this busted leg through a buckskin sling on the saddle . . ."

"You stay," stated Gunhill, straightening up to go fork down feed for the horse. At the foot of the loft-ladder he turned. "Jasper, there's one thing those women across the yard *don't* need, and that's to be left plumb alone. You understand me?"

Jasper understood, but he said, "Another thing they don't need, Phil, is for someone who's tryin' to help them to get killed doing it. Remember, this here ranch is in a bad spell of worse luck."

Gunhill almost smiled. "Well, for one thing I won't be *on* the ranch. For another thing, Jasper, those fellers won't know me from Adam's off ox, when I find them . . . And there's one other thing." Gunhill slapped the ivory-stocked Colt he was wearing. "I didn't just buckle this thing on day before yesterday." He started up the ladder hand over hand, leaving Jasper over there by the saddle-pole looking less distressed and more exasperated.

By the time Gunhill had fed the horse, had climbed back down and was finished choring for the day, someone over at the main-house rang the dinner-bell. Jasper straightened up, gripping his walking-stick.

Without a word he and Gunhill left the barn heading across the yard. Just before they reached the main-house, Jasper had a warning to offer.

"Don't mention none of this to the womenfolk. They'd never allow it. Especially Miz' Spencer. She's about beat down; the idea that someone might get hurt again, working for the Arrow iron, would put her into the same kind of slump she was in when her man died."

Gunhill nodded, and they resumed their stroll to the house.

6

When a man drifted, time and miles blurred, and since most drifters had no established goal, the blur became a continuum either marred or blessed by bad weather, good weather, convenience and pleasure, or inconvenience and displeasure.

Gunhill could guess mileage as well as the next man, normally, but when he left the Arrow yard well before sun-up the day he went up his back-trail looking for two thieves and fifty head of Arrow steers, he had trouble making a satisfactory estimate of the distance Arrow ranch was from the Laramie–Fort Collins road. The ride eastward before his horse had cast a shoe, had been pleasant; he'd had no destination, had allowed the horse to pick the route and gait, and subsequently, even if he hadn't left the yard in pitch darkness, which always made it hard to guess distances and sometimes compass points as well, Gunhill would not have had a very good idea of how much ground he had to cover.

The only compensating factor, he told the *grulla* gelding, was that from what he had been able to read off the drover's road the previous day, those two thieves were not pushing the stolen cattle. Perhaps they knew no one from Arrow ranch could find them, or back them down if they could find them. Perhaps they had in mind a local sale, and pushing cattle hard in the hot time of the year usually caused at the very least a five percent shrink. Everyone who had cattle to sell, even cattle thieves, wanted every last cent out of a critter that could be wrung out.

But whatever the reason for not pushing the animals hard, Gunhill was hopeful that once the thieves got near a town, they would not pick up the gait. He was also hopeful — and almost confident as well — that the thieves would not try to sell the Arrow cattle locally. Even as isolated and distant as Arrow ranch was, it was a reasonable bet that the people in places like Virginia Dale and Tie Siding knew the brand, and might even know the owners on sight. It was a risk no sensible rustler took if he could avoid it, and these two thieves simply had to head southward towards Fort Collins, or northward towards Laramie, to avoid that risk; no one in either of those larger towns would know either the Spencers or their brand.

As Gunhill rode hunched against the predawn cold, coat buttoned under his chin, hands encased in gloves, he very much wanted to believe the thieves would turn up-country, northward towards the Wyoming line and beyond, towards the Laramie plains, because this was the gamble Gunhill was taking; he was short-cutting through the hills on a course he estimated would put him beside the stage-road well north of Virginia Dale, north even of Tie Siding, up onto the southerly end of the Laramie plains, at least a day ahead of the driven cattle.

If the rustlers turned southward, Gunhill would be waiting for them up north, without a prayer of a chance of meeting them.

It was better not to think about that, but as he rode, hunched and stiff, he made a contingency plan. If the rustlers did not appear by the following evening, he would go down to the Siding, leave his horse at the liverybarn there, take the first coach through and try to beat the rustlers southward towards Fort Collins.

As long as a man did not think in terms of defeat, he would be just about impossible to defeat.

When the sun came, finally, the landfall was not familiar in detail, but it was familiar in its general formation. Gunhill was on the correct course. His instinctive, rangeman's inherent sense of direction had never failed him. It did not fail him now.

The warmth came slowly, and even after it finally arrived in full force, Gunhill continued to ride in gloves and coat for another couple of hours. By then, even the *grulla* was completely warmed-out.

They crossed as few topouts as possible, angling around every hill and slope they met in order not to have to slacken pace. They stopped once, shortly past high noon, in a virgin glade where brawling creekwater plunging southward from a snowfield somewhere higher up, was almost too cold to drink, and where the grass was strong, without being washy.

Gunhill loosened the cinch and let the horse graze free, as he rolled a smoke for his mid-day meal and hunkered in pine-shade while he estimated the distance they had come, and the distance they had yet to traverse. He came to the conclusion that, barring obstacles or accidents, they should be close to the stageroad by late nightfall.

There were some flat tins of sardines in

Gunhill's saddle pockets, an extra sack of Bull Durham, along with his tiny salt bag and the rolled up hooks and line he always carried in freshwater country. There were probably trout in the brawling whitewater creek, but he did not try catching any; it took time to build a fire, get rocks red-hot to cook fish upon, and time was the one thing he could not squander. Not now. A couple of days ago he could have squandered it by the bucketload.

As he doused the smoke and arose to go catch the *grulla,* he smiled whimsically to himself over the latest trick Fate, or Someone, had played on him. From a footloose wanderer to a man in a hurry with a definite destination in just a couple of days, was worth that kind of a private slow smile.

He left the clearing, skirted a stand of enormous pines, mostly over-ripe and ready to start declining, forded a second, shallower, more sluggish creek, and found a game-trail with bear-sign near a wild blueberry patch, which he followed warily because the bear-sign had been very fresh, and the surest way for a mounted man to end up on foot was to be dozing in the saddle when his horse rounded a bend and came face to face with a bear.

But the bear had evidently gone downhill,

because Gunhill did not see him, which was just as well for them both. Still, the *grulla* had the bear-scent in his nostrils and stepped along like a man walking on eggs for at least two miles after the last sign and smell had been close.

Finally, Gunhill rode down across a big, emerald park and came across the disarray and cast-offs left behind by a band of Indians. Remembering his earlier sighting of the Hidatsas, he wondered if this hadn't been one of their temporary halting places. It would have been fairly simple to make a determination, if Gunhill had cared to pause, but he simply made certain that when the redskins had departed, they, like the bear, had taken the route of least resistance, which was down-country, and kept on going until, upon the far side of the park, he passed into another cool, fragrant, and gloomy span of forest.

He started up a small band of elk. With the cows were several leggy youngsters and one ear-torn, face-scarred, roman-nosed old buck who covered the speedy, crashing withdrawal of his extensive family with a defiant stance and several warning snorts. Gunhill reined up and around the old bull, and laughed at the warning head-shake he got, passed beyond and when he looked back, the bull was eyeing Gunhill as though he simply could not understand why the mounted man had not stopped to give battle, or perhaps because he'd just received a big infusion of confidence, now that he had obviously routed one of those dangerous two-legged things.

Otherwise, though, Gunhill passed through all those miles of game-country without seeing much wildlife, and of course the reason for that, as he well knew, was that a man riding a shod horse made enough noise, even when he was passing over pine-needles, to warn off every living thing with acute hearing, within miles. *They* saw Gunhill, but *he* almost never saw *them.*

The land, though, did not change. It remained endlessly varied in topography, and yet always the same in its details; there were those hidden, beautiful parks, the craggier, stonier hills with forests covering them, the veiny little freshwater creeks, always running in low places, and always distantly visible from the heights, great mountains so distant they seemed to be mirages, because they blended so perfectly with the sky and heat-haze.

Finally, with the sun near to setting, Gunhill turned the horse straight up a long-spending gradual slope to the top of a wind-swept, gravelly ridge, and from that height, he saw on ahead where the land yielded on both sides to form a roughly north–south slot. It was familiar.

He rode down the far side of his hill and set a straight course due eastward. The stageroad ran down that slot.

A study of the sun's position was gratifying, in a way; he had bested his own estimate of how long it would take him to reach the stageroad. Not by much, though. By the time he finally passed around a cone-shaped hill and could see the roadway, dusk was settling. He still had a mile or more to go, it would be almost dark by the time he got out there.

The reason he had bettered his estimate was because he had not adhered to the northward route as much as he had thought he was doing. By several degrees, he had dropped southward. But that was all right; he was satisfied the thieves would not be this far north even though they had been on the trail at least three days. The drover's road which he had visited, southward from Arrow ranch, was quite a few miles below, southward.

When he finally began quartering for his night campsite, the horse helped; he was thirsty after the long afternoon ride through breathless heat, and scented-up a creek. Gunhill followed along it to the good area of grass, then swung off, hobbled the *grulla,* dumped his saddle, slipped off the bridle, washed the animal's back with creek-water from his hat, and when the *grulla* wanted to lie down and roll, Gunhill removed the hobbles until this necessity had been taken care of, all the itches had been scratched, then he replaced the hobbles and they eyed one another, the man understanding and kind, the horse honest and satisfied.

An hour later, having eaten one of his tins of sardines, Gunhill made a small fire to keep warm by, spread his blankets, and heard a horseshoe strike stone off through the shadows and trees on his right. He rolled clear of firelight, palmed the ivory-butted Colt, and waited. When the rider came through the trees, he called ahead.

"If you got meat, I got coffee."

Gunhill called back. "Ride on in." He remained away from the fire until the range-man appeared, halted and tiredly swung to the ground looking around. "Hell," he called to Gunhill, "if I'd wanted your money or your outfit, friend, I could have skunked you from back in them trees when I first saw your firelight."

Gunhill returned to the light, gun holstered. His guest was a wispy, greying man with a lined face, leathery skin, and saddle-warped legs. He made a swift assessment of Gunhill then turned to rummage in his pack for a tiny, two-cup coffee pot.

Gunhill stepped over to help with the unsaddling. "I don't have anything but a tin of sardines," he told the drifter, and got a typical retort from a man who was accustomed to existing on very little.

"All right with me, mister. You pitch in the little fishes and I'll pitch in the coffee."

As Gunhill eased the man's saddle to the ground, he said, "You came from the south?"

The warp-legged man replied while stepping to the creek to fill his little pot. "Yeah; hot down there below Fort Collins in the open country. I never could stand heat very good, so my horse and me decided we'd come up through here and maybe go over into the Wind River country until autumn."

Evidently the stranger was garrulous by nature, because when Gunhill asked his next question, he got another full and pungent reply.

Gunhill said, "See a small drive down-country a few miles, by any chance?"

"Yup. Two fellers drifting along a nice little bunch of up-graded animals, mostly got

Hereford blood. Steers. They was travelling lazy-like, for which a man can't fault 'em; this time of year you push a drive and you sure sweat off a lot of weight. I figured they was probably some local boys from in these hills somewhere, maybe in need of some cash-money, so they was trailing up to one of the towns on the Laramie plains. Maybe over to Cheyenne, or maybe to the soldier-fort beyond Laramie." The wispy man poured coffee from a little cotton sack with great care, set the pot atop some stones at the fire, and looked around where Gunhill was caring for the horse. "Where's them sardines?" he demanded.

7

Gunhill never told the grubline-rider his name and did not ask the older man's name. It was a casual meeting, a casual acquaintanceship, a passing in the night of rangemen, the same kind of easy meeting and relaxed association men encountered on working cow ranges or in bunkhouses; as long as a man behaved according to range-country social rules, he could call himself Abe Lincoln or King George if he wished to, and maybe he'd get slyly chided in good nature for it, but rangemen would trust him as long as they found him trustworthy; *that* mattered, names didn't.

The kind of association Gunhill had with that wispy, bandy-legged man was easy. They sat and talked, smoked, made a second pot of coffee, smoked and talked some more, then rolled into their bedrolls when the firewood was gone, along with the coffee, turned up onto their sides and went to sleep.

They awoke within ten minutes of each other in the cold, fishbelly-dawn, grumbled, scratched, looked out to be certain the horses were still around, hadn't caught panther-scent in the night and gone hopping in the opposite direction, and as they pulled on their boots they exchanged a greeting, then went to work making ready for the new day.

Gunhill turned the idea over in his mind about sending the rider down to Arrow for a riding job. He had no doubt but that the wiry man was a tophand. He had the tip missing on one finger to prove he'd roped a lot — and at least that one time he'd roped carelessly. His clothing, boots, spurs, bridle, even his worn saddle, showed more than enough use.

Gunhill was still toying with the idea when the wispy man, sipping hot coffee and smoking a cigarette for breakfast, said, "You know, mister, there's one advantage to havin' nothing. You can't get no poorer, can you? So — if you make out in *that* shape, why you just plain can't do no worse, and bein' satisfied in that shape, you don't have to do a damned thing you don't want to do. Like work. Now, for the balance of this summer and maybe into the autumn, me'n my horse just don't figure to do a blessed damned thing that don't strike our fancy. We'll go where we want, sleep when we want, get up when we want, and providin' I can shoot it, we'll eat what we want. You know any kings can do any better?"

Gunhill's slow smile started up. "I don't know very many kings."

"You know what I mean."

"Yeah, I know, and the answer is — no, I don't suppose you can improve on that. If that's what you really want to do. I started out that way last spring."

"Started out that way? You sound like you went to work."

"I did. For a cow outfit southwest of here quite a few miles."

The wispy man looked sympathetically over. "You see; you went and back-slid. Mister, you got to resist; you got to have an iron will." He flung aside coffee grounds, got to his feet and winked at Gunhill. "Well, partner, wish you was ridin' my way, we could team up and laze around a hundred camps and swap lies until winter."

The last Gunhill saw of this cowboy, was just before he angled away on his horse, passing into a spit of trees that hid the place where they had camped from the roadway.

They would never meet again, which was proper; rangemen were less like the tumble weeds folks said, than they were like the windblown leaves of autumn.

Gunhill walked out to look the *grulla* over, and got a reproachful, long-faced dolorous gaze. The *grulla* had no desire whatsoever to be hauled back, rigged out, and ridden. Even when Gunhill turned back to the camp, the *grulla* continued to eye him with suspicion. Even the very best of those smelly two-legged things couldn't let the sun rise and set without forking a horse's back.

Gunhill loafed. According to the passing rider those two thieves would not reach the state line, let alone the Laramie plains above it, until very late in the day, and if they didn't pick up the gait a little, they probably would not get up there until tomorrow morning. Meanwhile, Gunhill was out of food.

It did not worry him much. He could have ridden over to Tie Siding and bought tinned goods at the general store. He didn't for a very good reason; whatever came out of his eventual meeting with those sons of bitches who had deliberately stolen fifty prime animals from Arrow ranch because they thought there were only two helpless women to suffer the loss, if no one but the pair of rustlers ever saw the man who came down on them, then, in case someone got hurt or maybe even killed, the people who could identify Gunhill as having been around, would be only one or two, and those would be the thieves themselves.

Gunhill went fishing. He hiked a mile up the creek before finding a decent pool, and caught one fat speckled trout. He did that four times at four different pools; took one fish from each pool.

He returned to camp in early afternoon, gathered stones, stoked up his fire, and took his time at cooking the fat trout. A man could do it heaps faster with a fry-pan, but the number of rangeriders who packed fry-pans when they weren't travelling, were blessed few. Gunhill had a fry-pan — back in the bunkhouse at Arrow ranch, in his possible-sack, which did not do one damned bit of good where he now was, so he cooked his fish on the stones, ate one for a belated noon-day meal, wrapped the other cooked carcasses in tree-leaves and hid them from the scourge of every camp where there was meat — ravenous yellow-jackets, those blasted little flying varmints that were absolutely unheard of until a man brought forth meat of any kind, cooked or raw, then they appeared as though by magic. They could devour half a hanging deer in one night, right down to the glistening bones. And there was something else they could do — sting like they carried a red-hot poker.

Gunhill hid his meat, walked out to sit a while with the horse, whose suspicions returned all in a rush, again, and later, with the heat bringing on a lethargy, Gunhill sprawled in the shade and slept away nearly all the afternoon and the early evening.

He took a bath in the creek. Not because he particularly wanted a bath; the water was as cold as ice; but because he had the time to kill and there really wasn't much else to do. The sun's last rays dried him, he re-dressed, considered riding southward through the trees to find a ridge to watch the road from, decided not to make the horse do this, and, leaving his carbine and spurs at camp, *walked* several miles southward, with the sun dropping steadily lower, until he found the right hill to climb.

From the topout, breathing hard, Gunhill had a panoramic sighting of hundred of miles of broken, forested, unspoilt open country, but there were no cattle in sight and not even any dust to show that they might be somewhere farther south than he could see, and this worried him. If he'd brought the *grulla* he would perhaps have ridden farther southward, until he either saw the drive or caught sight of the men bedding their animals in a meadow and getting ready to set up camp. He didn't have the horse, and he was not going to do any more of that walking, so he turned back, not really too worried, but plagued by a small doubt. Maybe the thieves had left the road, knew a short-cut towards Laramie or Cheyenne, the same way Gunhill had ridden a short-cut to get ahead of them.

By the time he removed another of the cooked fish from his cache for supper, it was turning dark. It was then too late to saddle up and go manhunting, so he ate, smoked, and hoped with all his might his misgiving was incorrect; he wanted to see the drive coming in the morning. At the very latest, tomorrow afternoon. If he *didn't* see it, then he would indeed strike camp and go manhunting, regardless of what the *grulla* thought about it.

He lay under the stars for a long while, unable to sleep. Not from worry, especially; he was confident he'd find the men and the fifty steers with that arrow brand on their red-hided ribs; but because he had done nothing all this long day to make him sleep. Even that walk down-country and back hadn't been especially tiring. And he'd napped after his noon-day meal, too.

He thought about Jasper, about Gloryann Spencer, about her mother, and did not once think of the haunting things that had made him decide to ride alone all summer until he found himself again, and also found peace, so maybe he'd indeed found both.

Then he slept — and in the middle of the night the horse snorted and crow-hopped over closer to the man in the blankets, and that of course brought Gunhill straight up, gun in hand. It was either a bear or a panther. The horse told him that much from the way it was acting, and if the hobbles didn't hold, the horse would be ten miles away come sunup. But they would hold.

Gunhill had rid an area of pests before, under these same circumstances, by simply firing into some distant treetops. He did not raise his gun this time; a gunshot in the dead of a hushed, still night, was audible for many miles. The last thing Gunhill wanted was for those cattle thieves to think there might be someone up-country alongside the trail, waiting.

He rolled out swearing softly, pulled on his boots, took the carbine and went stamping out a short distance all around the camp. Whatever had frightened the horse had in turn evidently been frightened, because by the time Gunhill got back to his blanket-roll, the *grulla* was sufficiently calm to put that long-faced look of reproach upon the man.

Gunhill said, "Well hell, you darned fool, *I* didn't have anything to do with it."

The horse, though, did not wander very far from the man for the balance of this night. In the morning, before the sun arose, he was hanging close, still wearing that slightly accusing expression.

Gunhill ate another fish, decided that when he got back to Arrow he was going to ask for a decent meal, then went down to the creek to wash and drink. By the time the sun was up, he decided that he would not look the darned horse in the face, he'd simply bridle him, saddle him, and ride southward.

By mid-morning he was farther inland from the stage-road than he'd been before, so, when he breasted a knoll and saw a stagecoach go swinging past, he hardly heard its noise at all.

Then, finally, he saw the dust. Cattle-dust was different from horse-dust. It was also very different from stagecoach-dust. He picked his way prudently until it was possible to skirt a forested slope from the rear, come around to the sunshiny side, fade out in trees as he angled towards the higher elevations, and to eventually sit his saddle halfway up the hill, totally camouflaged in speckled tree shade and filtered sunlight, watching a slow, distant drive of fifty fat red-backed steers being pushing gently along by a pair of slouching horsemen.

He did not even remember that misgiving from the evening before as he sat like a statue, watching. The cattle were not foot-sore, and they picked grass as they walked along. Gunhill shook his head and confided in the *grulla* that if those men were experienced cattle thieves, they certainly weren't very smart ones. Then he waited until the drive had poked on past before continuing on around the sidehill to the rear of the hill before descending, and paralleling the drive northward for a short distance. Only when he had enough country between himself and the lazy little drive, did he boot the horse over into a lope, in order to get back and strike his camp before anyone could accidentally discover that a man had been waiting up there.

It was slightly past noon when he rode northward, up where the plains began and the trees and up-ended country fell away. This, the lowest end of the Laramie plains, would undoubtedly be where the thieves intended to bed down their drive tonight. No rangeman would ever bed cattle in hilly, forested — catamount — country, if he had a choice between that and open land.

Gunhill did not leave the hills, though. He set up a little dry-camp upon the northerly slopes, back in among some trees, and waited.

The drive did not arrive up there, beyond Gunhill's dry-camp, until shadows were beginning to puddle in the low places, but eventually it reached that vast sweep of prairie, and its drovers let the cattle sift out to the west a mile or two, once they were out of the rougher country.

Gunhill tried to count the animals, but between bad light and the way the steers bunched and intermingled, he never came up twice with the same figure. But it was close enough, so he spent the balance of the day watching the rustlers. They were both lean men, youthful, unshaven and unkempt, but they rode good horses, and they both carried two kinds of guns. Gunhill did not have to know much more. He went back, rolled into his blankets, made certain the grulla would not pick up the scent of those other horses a couple of miles ahead, then he bedded down, completely satisfied and confident.

8

Gunhill did not sleep very well, and before sunup he sat up, sniffed the night, then rolled out reaching for his boots. He had only a couple of miles to go, but crossing that open plain in daylight in the direction of a camp where a pair of cattle thieves were camping, was nothing he wanted to do very much, so he brought in the *grulla,* caught the dolorous expression and bleakly saddled up without facing the horse again. An odd thing about horses, and even cattle, that any rangeman learned if he was around a single, solitary one of them for any length of time; every blasted one of them had the identical personality of some person, some human being, a man had known in his lifetime. The *grulla* reminded Gunhill very strongly of a cousin of his who had not returned from the war. His cousin hadn't been lazy; he'd never been lazy, but he'd always acted as though having to do almost any kind of physical work was an imposition. He'd made people he'd worked for feel as though they'd ought to be ashamed of themselves. The *grulla* had this self-same personality, and it bothered Gunhill, who was not an iron-willed, hard-driving man around animals.

They left the hills, came down upon the warm plain, and for once the wind wasn't blowing out there; it might come later, after daylight also arrived, because if there was one thing a man could count on in this lifetime, if he was on the Laramie plains very long, it was wind. It add a third curse to every cowboy's twin curses — death and taxes. Wind.

He smelled the cattle long before he saw a single red hide. His horse also smelled them, and for an uneasy few moments Gunhill worried for fear the damned horse would also smell those other horses up there in the darkness, and nicker. But the *grulla* was silent, right up until Gunhill detected the faint, pungent scent of woodfire-coals, and swung down to stand a moment while he tugged off both gloves, unbuttoned his coat, and reached down to yank free the six-gun tie-down. Then, if the horse had had in mind nickering, Gunhill could have cut him off fast with a grip over the nostrils. But the horse allowed himself to be led along as though he too were a silent stalker, a fellow-conspirator. Later, Gunhill would have reason to eye the *grulla* and wag his head about this ugly, poor-coloured big stout beast, but right at the moment, as he stalked the rustler's camp, the horse was the least of his worries.

He walked up until he was sure the wood-ash smell could not be more than a dozen yards on ahead, then he stopped to bend down, hobble the horse, and continue on alone.

The outlaws had also hobbled their horses. Gunhill found both animals drowsing and slightly hunched against the pre-dawn chill. He got past without arousing either horse.

He also had the scent of the stolen cattle strongly in his face as he came in from the west, to the place where a slight, tell-tale glow indicated the cooking-fire had been the night before.

He drew the ivory-stocked Colt, moved up very carefully and silently, saw the lumps on each side of the fire, looked for their weapons, saw carbines in saddleboots but no sixguns, and knew that each rustler had his Colt in the blankets with him.

He got the Winchesters without rousing either rustler, then went round the camp like an Indian, to crouch southward. He pitched one carbine over the sleeping men to the grassland up above. One man came up instantly, tousled head rising with the speed of a striking snake, sixgun poised to fire. The second man stirred sluggishly, hoisted his head, looked, then hoisted his head a little higher as the cobwebs inside his head dissipated, and when this thief finally raised up enough, gun in hand, too, Gunhill spoke from down below, from the area of the feet of those two men.

"Don't move! Don't even *blink!*"

For three seconds the night was thick was menace, with deadly hush. Gunhill waited, gun aimed and cocked. Eventually he said, "Ease off the hammer and pitch those six-guns away. Slowly now. Slow and careful."

The rustlers had no choice. They did not see Gunhill, did not dare move their heads to search for him in the darkness. Each man flung away his Colt, then they turned very slowly, sitting up in the bedrolls. Both were fully dressed, except for hats, boots and gunbelts.

Gunhill had no difficulty making out the pale blobs of faces, but otherwise it was too dark to see very much. He said, "Roll out. Keep your damned hands in sight. Move slow and easy."

Again the rustlers obeyed because they had no alternative. They hadn't said a word and neither of them offered to speak now, as they reached for their hats, first, then their boots. Gunhill was watching the man with the instantaneous reflexes, the man who had awakened almost at the same moment that hurled Winchester had hit the ground. He was a dark-headed, hawkish-profiled man. He pulled on one boot, then, instead of pulling on the second boot, he shoved one arm inside it. Gunhill heeded the swift, shrill warning in his head and tried to call out, but the rustler was as fast as greased lightning. He had the little derringer out, cocked, and was swinging it to aim, when Gunhill fired from a distance of no more than a hundred feet. The rustler's belly-gun also went off. It spat a six inch gorge of red-orange flame, and the report was as loud as a sixgun. The thumb-sized bullet ploughed dirt and grass just beyond the end of the outlaw's bedroll. Gunhill's slug had already struck the man when he had yanked the trigger. As this man went down, hard hit, his companion rolled like a ball in the direction he had hurled his Colt.

Gunhill tracked the second man, fired in front of him, and the gout of prairie soil that burst upwards practically in the second outlaw's face, made the man recoil with instinctive dread.

It was over that fast. Gunhill said, "Get up on your feet," to the uninjured man, who obeyed a little unsteadily, twisting to see whether or not Gunhill meant to kill him. "Now walk back and kick that damned derringer away from your friend. *Move!*"

The outlaw went back, looked for the little gun, and kicked it. Then he stood gazing down at the man in the blankets.

"How bad?" asked Gunhill.

"Dead," replied the outlaw, without bending for a closer look. He stared a moment longer at his partner, then slowly turned away, in Gunhill's direction. "Who the hell are you? We got no money. We're just —"

"I know what you are," stated Gunhill. "Rustlers. Lousy cattle thieves."

The outlaw looked harder. "I never seen you before in my life. We got a bill of sale for these critters. It's right here in my pocket. If you'll hold the damned gun down, I'll show it to you."

"Show it to Jasper," stated Gunhill, "and to the Spencer women."

The lanky man blinked, and looked even more intently. "You come from — down there?"

"Yeah. I work for Arrow."

"Since when?"

"Since day before yesterday," stated Gunhill, and straightened to walk closer so he could make certain the man who had tried to kill him with one of those treacherous little hide-out guns, was indeed dead. As he moved closer, he motioned the other man off with his gun-barrel, as he did this he said, "You and your partner are damned fools. Anyone would know enough to sweat off some weight in exchange for putting a lot of miles between themselves and possible pursuit. You're greedy, mister, and that — just cost your friend his lousy life."

The pause in this statement by Gunhill was occasioned when he looked down, very briefly. He did not have to look any longer than that. No man survived being struck squarely over the heart with a .45 slug from a distance of no more than a hundred feet.

He holstered his sixgun and appraised his surviving prisoner. The nearest law that Gunhill knew about was up at Laramie. There might be a town marshal in Tie Siding, but he doubted it. Tie Siding was little more than a handful of tarpaper shacks with an occasional false-fronted narrow building. As he'd ridden by it last week, Gunhill had idly guessed that no more than possibly fifty people lived there, now that the railroad had been built and the need for a siding in this particular area has ceased to exist.

He had no intention of taking his prisoner and the dead man all the way to Laramie — and lose those fifty steers who would scatter to the four winds if left alone on the plain for very many days. As for the dead thief, it didn't matter much where he was taken.

Gunhill said, "What's your name?" and got a predictable reply.

"John Smith."

"All right, John Smith, lie flat down with your arms over your head, out front."

The cowboy said, "I don't carry no hide-out gun." He said it scornfully.

Gunhill pointed. "Down, you son of a bitch, before I break an arm for you."

John Smith got belly-down, stretched both arms, and as Gunhill moved in to step across the man, leaning to make the search, the prone man said, "It should have worked. Except for you, by gawd, it would have worked."

Gunhill found no weapon and stepped away. "Get up."

Off in the east the sky was paling. It was possible, finally, to make out the bedded cattle. They were not as scattered as they had been. Evidently, once they had filled up on prairie grass, they had bunched for the night; this was strange country to them.

Gunhill pointed. "What was his name?"

'Carl Webster," stated John Smith, and it was a believable name, this time.

"How long you fellers been partners?"

"Since just before we hired on at Arrow. We met over at Crow's Landing. He was from Idaho." John Smith lifted his head and put a narrow, assessing look upon Gunhill. "What you got in mind for me?"

"Take you back with the cattle and leave it up to Jasper."

John Smith's lips curled slightly. "I got a better idea. You interested in making a little money?"

Gunhill, believing Smith meant by selling the cattle, shook his head and glanced out where the hobbled horses of the outlaws had just seen the *grulla,* and were beginning to show interest.

Smith said, "Not the lousy steers. You interested in making a thousand dollars without even having to sweat for it?" He pointed. "Him. Webster. He's wanted over in Idaho for stopping a stage, taking off the mail pouch and killing a gunguard while he was doing it. He told me that himself, one night at Crow's Landing, when we got drunk."

Gunhill gazed at Smith, looked again at

the dead man half in his bedroll, then lifted an arm to gesture. "Go bring in your horses. We'll tie Webster across his saddle and take him back with us."

Smith resisted. "Hell; you take him back to Arrow, and you'll have to bury him. This kind of weather you can't keep folks above ground very long once they're dead. Let's take him up to Laramie. We could make that by tonight, if we leave the damned cattle, and up there the sheriff would —"

"Mister, you go out and bring in your horses," stated Gunhill, "and shut up. I don't want to hear another word out of you until I tell you to talk. You understand?"

John Smith's narrow face and close-set, raffish eyes made a slow, slow measurement of Phil Gunhill. In dawnlight he looked different, not as thick in daylight as he'd looked in the darkness; the coat had made him seem much heavier, much sturdier. Actually, he and John Smith were about the same weight, although Smith was leaner and Gunhill was shorter.

Then Smith turned and stalked away, heading for the horses, and Gunhill leaned to strip the blankets off the dead man for a closer look. Webster was dark. Not as dark nor as aquiline in his features as Jasper was, but darker by far than either John Smith, or than Gunhill was.

Not that it mattered. Nothing actually mattered where Carl Webster was concerned. Not any more. Otherwise, Gunhill found some tinned peaches and some tinned beef, and squatted with his back to the corpse to eat breakfast while he kept an eye upon the shockle-headed outlaw who was kneeling to remove the hobbles before bringing in the horses.

9

They came to an understanding. Gunhill passed over the lead-shank to the horse carrying the lashed-down dead man, emptied John Smith's carbine and shoved it back into the rustler's saddle-boot. He kept the two pistols, the shellbelts, as well as the dead man's derringer and Winchester. He would cheerfully have cached the lot. They were a needless added weight for the *grulla* horse, but he did not believe he'd be coming back this way again, and weapons were valuable; he did not want to simply leave them lying out there. Finally, then, he pointed out where the bedded cattle were beginning to stir.

"You and I are going to drive them back the way they came," he told the rustler. "They'll drive easy. It's all familiar backtrail to them. You stay where I can see you all the time. You can't out-run a bullet, so don't be foolish and make a break for it, even when we get back down there in the broken country. We'll both be watching the steers, John, but I'll also be watching you with one eye. Remember; don't try to slip into the trees or ride around a hillside. Keep over there on my right all the time."

Smith wanted to protest. He had the expression of a man who had something to say, perhaps a lot of things to say, but he must have been mindful of Gunhill's earlier admonition about only speaking when he was told to, because he sat and glowered and said nothing.

The lead-rope of his dead partner's horse was tied hard and fast round the saddle-horn, and although neither of Smith's hands were tied, he knew better than to even surreptitiously try to untie that rope and cast it off, and he most certainly could not make a break for it, with his dead partner back there lashed to the saddle, and his dead partner's damned horse tied to him like an anchor.

He did not really know Gunhill, but he knew he could shoot, and he also knew that Gunhill *would* shoot. Under the circumstances, that was all John Smith had to know.

The cattle were reluctant to be trailed before they'd had an opportunity to fill up after the long night, but Gunhill did not make a drive out of it as much as he made a 'drift' out of it. He and John Smith eased the cattle southward for an hour, until the sun was fully up, then, where the plain began to yield to the broken southerly country, they eased the drive over towards the stageroad. True to Gunhill's belief, the animals hiked dutifully to the roadway, got onto it and walked right along, heading back in the direction they came north only the day before. Fortunately, cattle are not querying beasts or they might have resisted turning about and going back the way they had just come.

John Smith, gazing to his left, over where the village of Tie Siding crouched beside the railroad right-of-way, broke Gunhill's imposed silence by saying, "Mister, you're going against the law. You're supposed to deliver law-breakers to the nearest lawman. The nearest *official* lawman."

Gunhill's answer was drawled. "I had no idea you were such a stickler for the letter of the law, Mister Smith. Or is it that you'd rather take your chances with a county sheriff than with Jasper down at the Arrow ranch, where range-law applies?"

Smith avoided answering by saying, "I told you, I got a bill of sale right here in my shirt pocket."

"Made out to you?"

"No, to Carl Webster. He told me he bought them cattle for cash money."

"Too bad Carl's dead," said Gunhill dryly. "Mister Smith, if I took you and Carl up to Laramie, him dead and you alive and me with nothing more to say than that I caught the pair of you rustling Arrow cattle, it'd be easy for you to tell them up there some cock-and-bull story about it all being Carl Webster's doings and you were just an innocent feller roped in by Webster. And you know what I think? I think they'd turn you loose. But we're not going up there. Mind that damned lead-horse and quit trying so hard to come up with something clever."

The outlaw returned to his previous deep silence for a while. As they drifted southward past the distant village of Tie Siding, which was on their left, he glanced over there, and Gunhill saw a flicker of faint hope in the outlaw's face, so he said, "You don't give up easy, do you? We're not going to the Siding either, so forget it."

They had no trouble with the livestock. An occasional animal would stray off the road to graze along parallel with the main herd, and now and then one of these animals would fall back, but regardless of the fact that a steer's homing instincts had been stunted early, he had just about as strong a herd-instinct as other cattle; when the drive went past, the hang-backs, fearful of being left behind, would lumber to catch up and join the band.

Gunhill anticipated no real trouble, not even when they got southward where the road ran down its slot in the broken country where the opportunities for the cattle to hide, to spook, increased greatly. Even if the steers hadn't known the way, they would not have been difficult to drive. Nearly all the scatterbrained Texas breeding had long ago been bred completely out of them. They were stolid, placid animals. Nor were they built for running. Gunhill, watching them plod along through the increasing morning heat, wondered how long it would be, how many more years, before western cowmen would be able to drive their animals with a staff and a stout pair of walking boots, and perhaps a trained dog, the way sheepherders did.

He was roused from this reverie by the unarmed rustler. "You're going to have it on your conscience, if you hand me over to Jasper. He's a gawdamn' one-third In'ian, and everybody knows they aren't even civilised, let alone decent."

"Not everybody," stated Gunhill. "I don't

know that about 'em."

"You'll be a murderer!"

Gunhill shrugged. "Maybe. It's sure something to think about, isn't it?" He smiled directly into the cow-thief's eyes. "What are you? I mean, besides being a cattle rustler, what are you? A liar, to start with."

"What do you mean?"

"John Smith . . . ? Hell, a little kid could do better than call himself John Smith. That's a lie and we both know it. But it's all right with me — John Smith. They can carve John Smith on your headboard for all I give a damn. But you see, I've got a theory about liars; a man who will lie will steal, and the Lord only knows what else he'll do. When you lied to me about your name, you cinched it. As far as I'm concerned, a man like you takes up a lot of room and eats a lot of food, that a decent human being could use. Jasper can swing you from the front barn-baulk for all I care. I'll even loan him my lariat to do it with."

John Smith rode along staring at Gunhill as though he were having difficulty understanding the man. Gunhill did not snarl, he did not even swear very much, and he was neither bitter nor cruel — and yet from what he had just said it was impossible not to believe that he would watch a man strangle ten feet off the ground dangling by the neck from a lariat, without feeling anything at all. *That* was the kind of a man John Smith should fear, and he slowly came to the full realisation of this. A man who growled and struck out with a fist, who swore a lot and ranted and threatened, was nowhere nearly as totally deadly as the soft-spoken, completely candid, sometimes gently smiling kind of man that Gunhill seemed to be.

The outlaw had been more startled than fearful back on the Laramie plains. Even after the slaying of his partner, he had been less afraid than conniving. But now, going inexorably back where he knew without a doubt what awaited him, or anyone else who broke the laws of the range, riding with a man to whom even the inducement of reward money meant nothing, was an increasingly withering, chilling, frightening experience.

Like all rangemen, as long as the outlaw had been active, had been able to lose himself in something he was doing and did not have to suddenly haul up short and *think,* life was agreeable, and living it was worthwhile. But now he had to poke along, unarmed, within gun-range of his captor, heading back where he would not have the chance of a snowball in hell.

He said, "Listen a minute. We got a long way to go and it ain't going to be easy once we leave this damned stageroad. Your chances of getting me back to Arrow ranch are going to get slimmer the farther we ride together. Why don't we work something out?"

Gunhill put a calm, impassive gaze upon the rustler. "Work what out?"

"If you got some reason for not wanting to go back up to Laramie with Carl and put in for the reward on him, then I figure you got a reason for not wanting to meet the law up there, and that's fine with me. I ain't exactly fond of the idea either. But you don't have to lose that five hundred dollar reward, neither."

Gunhill continued to stare. "Don't I? And you said about three, four hours ago, it was a thousand dollars."

"Yeah, well, you see, it's five hundred from one county over in Idaho, and five hundred from another county."

Gunhill sighed. "You aren't even a very good liar, are you?"

The outlaw ignored this to speak on, pushing out his words in a rush. "You can have both our outfits, including the guns and packs and horses and saddles. Mister, down at Fort Collins or over in Cheyenne, you could sell all that stuff for a lot of money."

Gunhill looped his reins and went to work making a cigarette. "And all I've got to do is turn you loose," he murmured. "Hell; I've already got the outfits." He lit up and stowed the tobacco sack. They rode along for a while in silence, then Gunhill said, "I'll tell you what I believe, Mister Smith. I believe that the man carrying the bill of sale to these cattle is the one who figured out how to steal them, and also how to fake a bill of sale to hand over to whoever bought them later. I also believe all that talk about Carl Webster being worth a reward over in Idaho doesn't fit the man back there tied across his saddle. I believe you're Carl Webster."

The outlaw reddened and glared, but for a few yards he said nothing, and Gunhill could see the resolve hardening on the man's face, down around his pinched, bloodless lips. Then the outlaw spoke again, finally, staring icily at his captor.

"You'n Jasper sure as hell better make it good, when we reach the ranch, cowboy."

In the same attitude of imperturbable calm he had shown towards his prisoner since they'd left the plains and headed into the broken country southward, Gunhill answered that frank threat.

"We'll make it good, don't you worry much about that."

It was Gunhill's intention to leave the stageroad in roughly the same area where he had first seen it on his short-cut ride from the ranch. This way, they would be able to reach Arrow ranch either late in the coming night or tomorrow. If they went back down south all the way to that old drover's road, and turned west down there, they would be at least three days on the trail, unless of course they pushed the cattle hard, and Gunhill knew better than to try that; these steers had been walking steadily for several days already. It wasn't the weight-loss that bothered him; they would begin getting tender-footed by tomorrow, and after another additional day or two on the trail, they would begin to drop out, too sore to do anything more than hunt up a creek-bank and stand in mud. He would not get the entire fifty head back to the ranch, and that was his sole objective in undertaking the pursuit in the first place.

As for John Smith–Carl Webster, or whatever his name was, Gunhill was not too concerned. He had no intention of helping Jasper hang the rustler, and he had no intention of witnessing any such attempt, but that was something he kept to himself. He knew the rustler was worried, and he had no objection at all to allowing him to go right on worrying. If Jasper wanted to take the outlaw over to Crow's Landing, Gunhill would do that much; it was on his way in any case. When he left Arrow ranch he might as well ride due west to the town as ride in any other direction.

Finally, there was one other consideration. He had no intention of hauling that corpse behind him for three days; he wanted to get him to Arrow ranch as quickly as possible, too.

10

The outlaw gave Gunhill a look of wonderment when they swung the steers off the stageroad southwesterly, in the direction of Arrow ranch. His opportunities for attempting an escape had just increased a hundredfold.

Gunhill caught that look and guessed what lay behind it. He said nothing for a couple of hours, until they had the steers settled in the direction they were supposed to travel. What made it a little more difficult now, was the fact that they occasionally had to keep the cattle bunched without losing any as they passed through the trees. Gunhill would ordinarily have scouted ahead for a route that might have avoided this. He could not do any such thing as long as he had to do most of the work, while at the same time keeping an eye on both the cattle and his prisoner. On the other hand, he had very recently covered this self-same area, and could think ahead with sufficient capability to avoid the worst stands of trees, which was in his favour. Another thing in his favour was the fact that he did not try to push the steers. He allowed them to graze along. He would have preferred to push them, but under the circumstances he'd have lost a few head, or they would have scattered under pressure and in the end he'd have had to sacrifice a lot of time bunching them again, which still amounted to the same thing — lost time.

He estimated the odds at fifty-fifty. Fifty chances that he *would* succeed against fifty chances that he would *not* succeed. He was willing to accept those odds, and while he mentioned none of this to his captive, he did tell the outlaw that anyone trying to make a break for it in this rough country, dragging a laden horse behind him, had about as much chance of making it as he had of flying to the moon, and the outlaw seemed to agree; at least he made no contrary comment and he rode along chousing an occasional drag-critter as though he too were interested in getting the steers back on Arrow range.

Time, Gunhill recognised, was not in his favour, and that just might be the element which would defeat him. But he had an antidote for that, too. If they were not back close enough to the ranch by nightfall for the steers to be left on their own, to be found tomorrow morning and brought the rest of the way on in, Gunhill would simply let the cattle bed down in one of the many parks in this area, tie his prisoner to a tree, and sit up until dawn.

Once, when the rustler said, "You got a lot of faith in yourself, mister," Gunhill answered a trifle shortly. "Not in myself. In my ability to shoot fast and straight."

That was the kind of a retort the cow-thief understood. He poked along, keeping the cattle moving, occasionally turning to swear at the led-horse behind him.

They got well down through the swales and tree-fringes, always following out the low, wide little arroyos which the steers preferred to utilise rather than climb hills or wander in the pine-woods, because there was grass only in those wide swales, before they came to a coldwater-creek. The cattle lined up, muddying the water to noisily drink, and the outlaw, who was also thirsty, cursed them for this.

Gunhill took him north of the milling steers, let him get down and drink, then he drank himself, and watered all three horses. Finally, since it was nearing high noon, he rolled two smokes and passed one up to his mounted captive from the ground. While he stood there offering a light, which the outlaw leaned down to utilise, Gunhill said, "Where are you from, Carl; Idaho?"

The outlaw did not deliberately fall into the trap, but he acknowledged the truth of it by straightening up and looking at Gunhill with a bitter little smile. "Yeah, Idaho and other places. And I reckon it don't make much difference about the name. Yeah, I'm Carl Webster."

"What was *his* name?"

The rustler cast an indifferent glance over one shoulder at the lashed-down dead man. "I don't know. He called himself Tom Jennings and said he was the nephew of the train-robber and bank-holdup-man Al Jennings. I don't know about that either."

"Where did you meet him?"

"Over in Crow's Landing in the saloon. We was both looking for a riding job. A freighter over there told us we'd ought to ride inland to the Arrow place, that he'd heard the boss over there was sick, and figured they might need a couple of rangemen."

"That's all you know about him?"

Webster sighed. "No. One other thing; he was about as fast a moving man as I ever knew. He was always coiled up like a spring. Well; you saw how fast he could react, back there on the plain. I just naturally figured a man who was that tight-wound would be damned fast with a gun."

"Rangeriders don't have to be fast with weapons," said Gunhill, and Carl studied him a moment, then quirked up his lips in a cold small grin.

"They sure don't. You caught me on that one. But then I didn't figure on us having to be rangeriders for ever, either."

"You figured to rob the Spencer ranch?"

Webster considered his answer shortly before offering it. "Not exactly. I just figured that sooner or later we'd run onto something. A man always does, if he keeps his eyes open and his ear to the ground. Maybe at the Arrow outfit, maybe somewhere else. We talked a lot, him and me, as we was riding inland. Tom was plumb willing. But I don't think he'd ever done anything before, at least nothing like I'd done, because he kept asking the kind of questions a feller asks if he's a mite worried, a mite doubtful."

Gunhill smoked, stood in the shade, glanced southward where the cattle were mostly tanked up and had forded to the grassland on the far side of the creek, then, as he strolled back to his horse, he asked another question.

"What in the hell made you think you could get away clean with these steers?"

Webster countered with a question of his own. "Why not? There wasn't no one at the ranch but Jasper and the two womenfolk, and the damned Arrow livestock was scattered all through those parks out there. Even if Jasper rode every day, he wouldn't miss just fifty head of steers. Not for maybe a week or two, and by then they'd be hanging on meat-hooks somewhere. That ain't a one-man ranch." Webster paused, stared southward at the steers for a moment, then said, "Say, how *did* they know them damned steers was gone?"

Gunhill stepped up across leather before replying. "I think the girl discovered they were gone. Jasper broke his leg while they were marking and the girl took over the range-riding. She took it seriously. I think you're probably right, about Jasper — about any average cowboy — he wouldn't go round with a pencil and a talley-sheet in his hand every day, counting horns. But the girl was just exactly that zealous."

Webster scowled. "That — what?"

"Zealous. She was that — dedicated, that efficient."

"Oh."

They rode back down, splashed across the creek and began easing the cattle along again. Webster said, "Say, did you go to school?"

Gunhill laughed. "Some. Why?"

"The way you use words like — zeelits."

"I studied for the ministry," said Gunhill, and saw the shock come over his prisoner's face. Webster stared, then he swore. "I'll be damned to hell. You're a lousy *preacher?*"

"No. I almost was, but I met a man who was a lot wiser than I'll ever be. He got the kinks out of me." Gunhill regarded Webster. "Forget it. We could talk about this for a week and never come together, so forget it."

Webster was agreeable to that. "Yeah. My gawd, if Tom was alive, I'd never live this down. Caught by a lousy preacher."

They had to turn the cattle twice, to avoid grass slopes, but it seemed to Gunhill that they were making fair time despite this, and their slow gait. If he'd dared push the animals he was now confident that he could make it all the way back to Arrow range before midnight. He was not tempted, though, so they poked along, and an hour after they'd left the grassy sidehills and were riding down through an angling, southwesterly slot among some bald hills, with thin tree-stands close by, Webster, eyeing the slanting sun, shook his head a little hopefully.

"You're going to lose them in the dark, mister," he exclaimed. "The first scent they get of bear or panthers or wolves, and you'll have steers scattered from here to hell and back."

Gunhill said, "You hope it ends like that, anyway. But I'll still have you, Carl. I can find the cattle again. I found them before." He looked at the outlaw. "If you'd come up this way, maybe you'd have been a little harder for me to overtake."

"That's exactly why we *didn't* come up through here. Tom and me saw plenty of wolf-sign and bear tracks when we rode for Arrow ranch. We figured it out; we'd have to go slow, and we'd have to get over onto the road so's the varmints wouldn't stampede the animals. Ordinarily, we would have figured we couldn't make it, having to waste so much time, but the way things was at the ranch, we knew we *could* make it. And by gawd we would have, too, if you hadn't come along and stuck your big long beak in."

"If I hadn't come along, Carl, you and your friend would have come back."

Evidently this idea had not crossed the

rustler's mind. He stared, then he said, "Maybe. If we'd thought about it, we might have."

"Sure you would have," stated Gunhill. "How many rustlers find a ranch where the owner is dead, where the only rider is laid up with a busted leg, and where there are only two women to look after several hundred head of fat, breedy cattle? The idea would have come to you, maybe when you and Tom were having a drink over in Cheyenne after you'd been paid for the fifty steers."

Webster did not argue, he said, "Gunhill, you gave up preaching?"

"I told you — I never was a preacher."

"Well; all right. Anyway, you got that silly stuff out of your head and went to range-riding. Now my idea is this; if you give up that silly crap and went back to makin' a living like a man — it shouldn't be too damned hard for you to make another shift . . . Listenin' to you just now, saying what Tom and me would have done, struck me as being damned wise."

Gunhill said, "Thanks," very sarcastically.

Webster ignored the interruption to press onward with his idea. "A man like you, who thinks ahead and who understands people, even without no experience, could team up with someone who knows all the ropes, and by gawd you could retire in a few years, a rich man, maybe even with a ranch of your own somewhere, and a nice big herd of graded-up critters that wouldn't cost you a lousy cent."

"That 'someone' I could team up with, Carl, who knows all the ropes, would of course be you?"

The outlaw moved his hands wide, palms up. "No other feller but. You interested? We could work the ranges and the stageroads from Montana south. This here is summer, the best time of year for our kind of work. I tell you —"

"This experience you have," stated Gunhill, breaking in, "just how much of it have you had?"

Webster warmed to the subject. "Plenty of it. Take my word for it, Gunhill, I've had plenty of experience at all kinds of it."

"Stages?"

"Yeah. I've stopped my share of them."

"And rustling?"

"Plenty of that too."

"And you've been at this for some years, Carl?"

"Off and on, I'd say no less than about eight years."

Gunhill looked stonily at the outlaw. "And

here you are, with a horse, a worn saddle, scuffed boots, and a dead friend tied to you, to show for all that experience and all those easy pickings." Gunhill shook his head slowly. "No thanks."

Webster, let down after what he'd hoped might have been at least a wavering on Gunhill's part, glared cold hatred at his captor, then turned and concentrated on driving the steers for a full hour without uttering another sound, or even looking over to see where Gunhill was.

The shadows were getting close, the sun was steadily dropping, the heat, which had been noticeable in the middle of the afternoon, was slightly ameliorated now, where sunlight no longer could reach, and the steers were beginning to act as though they wanted to stop and spread out for their final couple of hours of daylight grazing.

Gunhill thought they were still about four hours from the ranch, and perhaps about an hour from Arrow range. He began to believe he was going to make it back without difficulty after all.

11

The gunshot came with such suddenness that even the cattle, by nature acutely anticipatory to anything loud and unexpected, were stunned into immobility. Then their muscles and nerves began to react, and if there had been another such sudden, deafening explosion, they would have stampeded in every direction.

But there was no second shot.

Gunhill reacted to the sound in the way the cattle should have reacted, except that the cattle had just filled up with water, were sluggish, and were tired from their day-long walk. Gunhill went off the near-side of his *grulla* horse streaking for his Colt. He put the horse between himself and the upland little spit of forest where a faintly discernible wisp of soiled, burnt powder drifted. It was too great a distance. Gunhill put up the Colt and hauled forth his Winchester to place it lightly across the saddle-seat.

There was not a sound, except for some of the steers moving off a little ways, uneasily sniffing that burnt gunpowder. Even the treetop-birds were still, which was something a gunshot could accomplish unwittingly anywhere one sounded; not only the birds, but any four-legged animals within earshot, turned cautious and motionless and fearful, as they listened and looked.

Gunhill turned to see whether Webster had left the saddle too. He had. Carl Webster was nowhere in sight!

Gunhill threw a last, searching look over where the gunfire had erupted, then moved swiftly under the neck of Webster's horse and northward, still lugging the carbine. He crossed a dozen yards of open grassland-park, then encountered trees. Up to the first age-old thickness of pine needles, it had been easy to follow the fleeing outlaw's route. Booted feet slamming down hard as Webster had run for his life, had crushed grass with each stride, but in among the trees it was a different story. There had been no rainfall to soften the needles. They were not only brittle, they were also redolent of resin; something no one wearing leather-soled boots could run across very long before their soles got as slick as glass.

Gunhill was mad enough to shoot on

sight, but there was no outlaw to aim at. He had to follow the outlaw's tracks a foot at a time, and he did not have to go very far in among the trees before he realised what a losing proposition this was. Webster was making those tracks as fast as he could run, and Gunhill was following them as slowly as he could walk. The distance was steadily widening, nightfall was only a couple of hours off; all the rustler had to do was keep moving in the damned trees until dusk arrived, and Gunhill would be unable to do anything at all towards finding him until morning.

Webster was on foot in an immense, primeval land, which was certainly not a very desirable condition, but at least he was free, and he was still alive, and if those factors were cannily utilised, he could sooner or later steal a horse somewhere.

Gunhill walked back out of the trees as angry as a hornet, but when he saw the cattle beginning to settle in, beginning to bed down, even though there were still a couple of hours of good daylight yet, he consoled himself with the thought that he at least still had the steers, which was, after all, the only thing he had really ridden so far and hard, to find and return with.

Then he saw the lean, wide-legged stance

of the individual leaning on the carbine, standing a yard or so away from the *grulla* horse's head. He faltered in stride only a second; if that blasted damned gunshooting idiot over there had intended to shoot Gunhill, it could have been done any time within the last ten minutes, as soon as Gunhill had stepped from the forest to walk along, completely exposed and unprotected.

He stalked along, his anger re-kindling a little, but the real fury of it was well past by the time he stopped on the far side of the led-horse, where the corpse was lashed, and recognised the rifle*man.*

Gloryann Spencer!

She was white in the face. Her violet eyes looked almost black. She had come down there, out of the trees, and had walked right up to what she'd thought was a packed trail-horse, only to discover that the lumpy load was not a pack at all, it was a dead man.

She stared at Gunhill while he resumed stalking her. Without a word he leaned, took hold of her Winchester, wrenched it away and tossed it behind him in the grass. Then he said, "What in the hell are you doing out here, anyway? Didn't you see that prisoner I had on the other horse? You confounded simpleton, you fixed it so that he escaped up into the darned forest. What the hell did you fire for, anyway!"

She did not seem nearly as phased by his anger as she still was by the sight of that dead man. She turned, without changing expression, set her back to the led-horse, and pointed. "There; below that big creek-willow tree," she murmured. "I saw him crouching on the lowest limb from up the slope. If I'd waited another minute, the cattle would have been stampeded — all but the one he'd have landed on."

Gunhill twisted, saw the tree, saw nothing else and glared. "What are you talking about?"

She stepped past him, stepped over the carbine he'd taken from her and hurled in the grass, walked on over to the creek and halted, looking down.

It was the largest cougar Phil Gunhill had ever seen in his entire lifetime. From nose to tip of his tail, the big, sleek, incredibly durable and powerful cat measured eleven feet. His paws were half again as large as Gunhill's spread hands. He was shot through the body, well forward.

From a kneeling position, Gunhill lifted his head and looked southeastward, up that slope where Gloryann had fired from. It was a very long distance for a carbine to reach, and even more unbelievable, at that distance the bullet should have been adversely affected by both windage and droppage.

Luck, he told himself, arising to stare at the huge cat.

The girl with the cornflower-coloured eyes said, "Well . . . ?"

Gunhill slanted a look at her. She was standing like a ramrod, looking at him from a face made cold by leashed fury. He concentrated upon the big dead cat. "Quite a shot, from up where you were in the trees."

She continued to glare.

He grounded his carbine and leaned upon it, turning slowly. "I said more than I should have," he admitted lamely. "Still, that shot made me lose my captive."

"You got the cattle back, didn't you?"

"Yes; but there was a little unpleasantness on the plains south and west of Laramie. That one tied on the horse got killed. The other one — I was bringing them both back to the ranch."

"The *cattle* are what we wanted back, Mr Gunhill. We certainly didn't want a — corpse — and what would we do with that one that got away from you up in the trees? We don't even have a root-cellar to lock him in until the law from Crow's Landing could come for him."

His anger stirred a little, deep down. "Do

you think I should have just left him free, up there on the plain? That man has robbed stages and rustled cattle. He's been an outlaw for eight years. He told me that, himself. You think a man like that should be left running loose?"

She turned away from the dead cat, looked over where the cattle were drowsing, and said, "He *is* loose, isn't he?" Then, before he could shoot back an answer to that, she said, "I'll get my horse. I left him in the trees, and we can at least push the steers another three or four miles before it gets dark."

He said nothing. As she swung past, walking with her customary purposeful, lithe stride, he watched her go, and sighed under his breath.

Then it hit him! She was not limping and she was not favouring her side where the cracked or broken ribs were supposed to be. He watched until she disappeared up into the yonder trees, then sauntered over to the *grulla,* shoved the carbine into its boot, looked northward where Webster had disappeared, and where Webster was still no doubt trotting right along, then he thumbed back his hat, turned, and watched Gloryann ride down out of the trees towards him.

When she came up and halted, he said,

"You know, day before yesterday you couldn't walk and it hurt every time you drew down a breath. I've heard of miracles, but this is the only time I've ever *seen* one."

She reddened, slowly turned, splashed across the creek and called in a crooning way until she had the steers up onto their feet, then she began driving them.

Gunhill had two horses to lead. He would cheerfully have dumped the rigging off them both and freed them, except for the dead man. Tom Jennings, or whatever his name had been, was proving more obnoxious in death than he would have been to Gunhill if he'd still been alive.

Gloryann was good with cattle and she rode a horse as well as any long-legged, lean-built cowboy Gunhill had ever ridden with. He grudgingly gave her credit for that, but not aloud, only to himself. She was not riding that horse she'd been straddling when she'd roped the cow and had got jerked down. This time, the animal was a short-backed, muscular, skimpy-maned and skimpy-tailed grey. Gunhill had seen that kind before; Texans bred them for their cow-savvy. They were ideal range horses, but generally, they were about as comfortable to ride as a jack-hammer.

Gradually, Gloryann got the steers to

increase their gait. Gunhill had misgivings, but he said nothing; after all, they were *her* critters. Hers and her mother's critters, anyway. He hoped, too, that she'd get them hot and resentful so they'd either sulk on her or would scatter towards the trees. They did neither, although now and then a steer would show signs of wanting to do something like that. But Gloryann and the short-backed, rat-tailed grey gelding had a knack of being right there, when a steer began sidling away.

Gunhill shook his head. She had cow-savvy, no doubt of that. It pained him to admit it, even to himself, but she had as much cow-savvy as most rangeriders had. It was a bitter pill for a rangeman to have to swallow, but Gunhill gave even the devil his due.

She did not come back where he was pushing the drag until they were upon the first of the wide, emerald meadows. Even then, she did not actually ride back, she pulled up on the trail and sat there until he came along. Then she looked coolly at him.

"We're on Arrow range, *Mr* Gunhill. It'll be dark in a half hour. The critters are leg-weary. They're not going anywhere between dark and dawn. We can come back and pick them up after sunup, and drive them the rest of the way."

This, incidentally, was exactly why rangeriders objected to working for women-owners; they did not like being ordered about by females, and they most certainly did not like having women do their thinking for them. Right or wrong. Cow-country was *man's*-country. Women and horses were necessary in it, just like grass and water, with the essential difference being that grass and water and horses had a place and did not get out of it.

Still, Gunhill *had* been hard on her. Some of his anger had been justified, but not all of it, and Gunhill was an honest man with himself and with others; he *knew* that he owed her an apology — sort of.

As they sat in the soft gloaming he forced himself to say, "You're handy. You're good on a horse . . . I'm sorry I lost my temper back there. All I knew was that someone up in the timber cut loose with a Winchester, and I had an outlaw on my hands, plus fifty steers. Still, I shouldn't have said as much as I did say." He swallowed. "I apologise."

She did not loosen in the saddle, but she *did* look away, as though she was embarrassed. When she spoke, though, her voice was softer. "I — *had* to shoot the big cat. If I hadn't, we'd have been two weeks finding these steers again. But maybe if I'd just busted out of the trees yelling at the top of my voice, it would have scairt him off."

Gunhill had doubts about *that,* but he kept them to himself; he did not want to start another argument. Still, running at an oversized, fighting panther, yelling, wasn't something anyone who knew much about mountain lions would have advocated. Depending upon the cougar, a person could get badly clawed and bitten, and perhaps even killed, trying to brace such a varmint, without using a gun.

Gunhill sighed, looped his reins and started to make a smoke. As he lit up, trailing smoke in the still evening air, he looked northward. Carl Webster would be up there somewhere, breathless no doubt, but laughing to himself about how he had escaped. Damn him!

12

Gloryann suprised Gunhill by not suggesting that they head on down to the ranch. She surprised him further by taking him over to a small creek that seemed to spill straight out of a crevice in living granite. Over there, with the cattle dimly in sight, she dismounted, hobbled her horse, off-saddled, and without a word off-bridled the grey, then, with her back to Gunhill, who was caring for his own horse, the big, ugly *grulla* gelding, she dug in her saddlebags, brought forth one of those tiny two-cup enamelware coffee pots, a fry-pan, and several napkin-wrapped bundles. She knelt over there working with experienced hands, and when he strolled closer, she threw him a request, without actually lifting her face.

"We'll need some wood for the fire, Mr Gunhill."

He had to jump the creek and walk to the first slope where there was timber, to round up an armload of deadfall, dry wood, and hike back with it. She'd built a little, professional-looking stone-ring, and was ready when he knelt to shave kindling. He looked over. She had a huge steak, a much smaller steak, some potatoes which had already been sliced paper-thin, and the coffeepot was ready to be placed next to the fire. He concentrated on the wood, saying nothing, but he *was* hungry. The last bit of food he'd eaten had been on the plain southwest of Laramie, over near Tie Siding, and that was one hell of a long way from where he now was, and a lot of hours ago.

She waited, rocking back on her knees, until he had the fire going, then she started cooking. Only once did she raise her violet eyes, and that was when he sighed over the size of the big steak. She smiled. "I knew I'd find you when I left home before dawn this morning. That is, I knew I'd find you if you'd found the cattle and were on your way back. I thought you might be hungry."

He continued to watch the steak as it began sizzling when he spoke. "If you hadn't found me, all you'd have had to do for me to find you, was put that steak over a fire."

He looked over at her, slowly smiling. She flashed him a look, then became very busy at the fire. For a while she said nothing, and meanwhile, shadows came down around a hill north and west of their camp, bringing on the bland, fragrant promise of a warm mid-summer night.

When Gunhill tossed down his hat and washed at the creek, then rolled a smoke and sat opposite her, cross-legged, she said, "You had a right to be mad."

He studied cigarette ash thinking to himself that he was *not* going to bring *that* subject back again. Slowly drifting his eyes over to her, he asked a question in a very mild tone of voice.

"How are your ribs and your ankle?"

She reddened, but he could not discern it. All he noticed was how her full lips pulled flat, just a little, as though this happened to be a topic *she* did not want to discuss, and that, of course, made them even; they had both touched upon something the other one would just as soon not have touched upon.

Instead of answering, she pointedly said, "Jasper told me to take some salt, and bandage-rags. Jasper always seems to know how something will turn out." She looked up, finally. "What happened, Mr Gunhill?"

"You mean the dead man? He had a belly-gun hidden in his boot and went for it. He was fast."

"But you were faster?"

Gunhill shrugged about that. "We'll never really know about that, Gloryann. All I can tell you is that he was fast — but I already had my gun cocked and aimed at him. He didn't have to try that."

"What about the other one?"

"He didn't have a belly-gun, and he'd already pitched his sixgun away. I brought back all their weapons; they're by my saddle."

"Why didn't you and the other man bury this dead one?"

Gunhill said, "What with? I reckon we could have piled rocks on him the way the Indians do, sometimes, but that's a mighty poor way to bury a man. The ground is hard this time of year. Even if I'd had a shovel, I'd have had trouble digging a hole for him. Do you figure I should have left him lying up there on the plain?"

"No. I suppose you did the right thing."

He looked across at her from a mildly cynical face. "That's right kind of you."

She swept her eyes upwards again, and laughed quietly at his sarcasm. His slow smile came up; for a moment they looked steadily at one another, then she had to turn his steak, so she looked away, but he didn't. Gunhill began to sense a little change in himself; a kind of uncomfortable sensation.

It made him uneasy and restless. He looked over where the horses were, by the creek, and closer, where the saddles had been dumped. Tom Jennings was over there, too, which made Gunhill dislike the man more in death than he'd disliked him in life. Then Gloryann said, "Cougars usually travel in pairs, this time of year. That was a tom I shot, so the female might be around."

Gunhill was not worried. "She'll scent him up, find his body, and leave the country." He wrinkled his nose when the coffee came to a boil so she poured him a cupful, then she fished for a tin plate in her saddlebags, slid his steaming steak on the plate, allowing it to hang over on both sides, and handed it over with two hands.

He said, "Sure glad you happened along."

Her answer was short. "I didn't *happen* along."

He fished forth his pocket knife and went to work on the steak. He didn't give a damn whether she'd happened along, had come deliberately, had dropped from the sky or had popped up from the bowels of the earth, just as long as she had arrived, with that delicious steak and the means for cooking it. When he rolled his eyes, she laughed, looking very pleased. She held out a hand.

"Salt."

Their hands touched, their eyes met, and the word on his lips — “thanks” — got lost. They both held the tiny salt shaker until she recoiled quickly, and became very busy cooking her own steak. She could not fry his potatoes while she’d cooked his steak because there was insufficient room in the fry-pan, but she could fry them with her much smaller steak, and this fresh, tantalising aroma made him say, “You know, Gloryann, I’ve eaten in a lot of cafes and hotels, and even ranch-house kitchens, where the meal wasn’t half as good as this one is.”

She did not respond, but she listened, and afterwards her full, heavy lips were curved in an expression of soft pleasure.

He ate the entire steak, all his share of the potatoes, and drank two cups of coffee, then he rocked back in the grass and groaned, which made her show pleasure by laughing at him from across the tiny cooking fire. When he rolled his head and looked at her, she appeared in the diminishing firelight as a lithe young girl, no more than perhaps fourteen or fifteen. She also appeared, in another way, as a woman whose dark eyes showed an ancient promise, and whose smiling lips were formed for a lilting sound of something sweet, something tender.

But she kept silent.

She knew he was looking at her; even if she hadn't swept a glance over in his direction, she would have been able to *feel* his gaze.

Overhead, a warped old coppery moon hung in one place so long it seemed unable to move. The night was bland, warm, full of the delicate scents of cooling earth, cooling rocks, tree-sap which would congeal between now and morning, and the more difficult to define, haunting fragrance of brush, and shy small wildflowers in their shaded places.

Finally, Gunhill said, "Well, I had no idea it would end like *this*."

Her eyes flashed to his face. "Like what?"

"The steak, the fried spuds, the coffee. They were as —"

"Yes, I know," she broke in to say quickly. "As good as anything you've eaten in a cafe or a hotel." She began scouring the fry-pan with pulled swatches of grass and he watched. She was muscular, and where she knelt, over there, the curve of faded riding trousers lay taut around the full, strong roundness of sturdy legs. Her waist was so small he thought he could probably lock both hands around it. But she was a woman; even in the poor light, no man could ever have thought otherwise. She was a woman from her small, broad feet, to the crown of her copper-streaked, close-cropped blonde head.

He suddenly said, "Gloryann, why aren't you married?"

She increased the vigour of her fry-pan scrubbing as she replied, a little tartly. "To whom? We're thirty miles from the nearest town."

"But you *do* go over there, once in a while, don't you?"

She rocked back, looking at him. "Of course I go over there. Three or four times a year. What should I do — print up a sign and wear it on my back saying I'm Gloryann Spencer, I'm twenty years old, can ride well, can shoot well, know how to cook and darn and brand and —"

"Lady, you wouldn't have to do a darned thing but sit on a wagon-seat," Gunhill said quietly, raising up to prop his head on one arm, watching her.

She had an answer for that, too. "Evidently I *do* have to do more than that, Mr Gunhill. I'm still unmarried, aren't I, and have you noticed any long line of rangemen riding across our yard?"

"They just don't know you're here, is all, Gloryann."

She continued to sit back, hands on her

upper legs, looking at him. "*You* know I'm here," she said, and did not drop her eyes nor change her expression, nor even fidget with her hands.

Gunhill was nonplussed. He looked at the fire, looked over where the horses had not moved since the last time he'd looked over there, then he sat up and fished for the makings in order to have something to be occupied with until the discomfort, the embarrassment, the uneasy, bad feeling, went away.

Finally, he said, "Yeah, I know you're there, but I'm old enough to be your father."

"You are no such a thing, Phil Gunhill. You're not thirty. I'm twenty. Do you know much difference there was between my mother and father?"

He sought frantically for a way clear of this conversation, but failed to find one, so he lamely smiled and smoked, and poked into the ashes with a short stick, feeling almost as foolish as his smile looked.

She said, "Ten years. The same difference I think there is between your age and my age."

She was also a pretty fair judge of ages. He said so, a trifle weakly, and she came right back again. "Jasper told me you were about thirty. I didn't have any idea."

He had his first unkind thought about Jasper, then he got extricated from this dilemma, but in a way he would never have chosen.

A voice, speaking from the darkness over where the nearest low hill blended with the darkness by the saddles, said, "Don't you move, Gunhill, gawd damn you!"

Gunhill didn't move, but Gloryann's head jerked as though she'd been stung. She was staring intently over beyond Gunhill at something low in the grass over there. Very quietly, she said, "He's got a carbine."

Gunhill knew he couldn't have one of the pistols; they were unloaded and they were shoved down inside one of Gunhill's saddle-pockets. But the carbine, which *was* loaded, had been lying carelessly where Gunhill had dumped his saddle.

He heard the hammer slide back, oiled steel brushing over oiled steel. He could almost feel the sights of his own Winchester lining up on his back. He said, "You don't need the gun, Carl."

Webster called back an immediate reply to that. "Not after you fling that ivory-handled Colt of yours back here, I don't. Throw it, Gunhill! Throw it *left-handed!*"

It was awkward, the way Gunhill was sitting, to reach across, yank the tie-down loose, lift out the gun and fling it backwards, but if he hadn't obeyed, it would have been a hell of a lot more awkward trying to recover from a .30-.30 bullet between the shoulderblades, something extremely few human beings had ever been able to recover from.

Gloryann was Gunhill's only way of telling what Webster was doing back there. When she tilted her head, he knew Carl Webster was rising up off the ground. When she widened her eyes, he knew Webster was stalking forward.

13

It did not occur to Gunhill that the outlaw had something in mind other than perhaps vengeance against his former captor, the killer of his partner, and the redemption of his saddle horse, until he saw Webster's face as the outlaw stepped around to Gloryann's side of the diminishing little fire.

The outlaw was famished. Hunger was driving him, and now that Gunhill had recovered from his surprise and had time to reflect upon it, he became convinced that for as long as it had taken the outlaw to stealthily and very slowly stalk Gunhill and the girl, then, after dark, to belly-crawl a foot at a time towards the pile of saddlery where the guns were, Webster had had the tantalising fragrance of all that cooking food to increase his food-craving.

Now, the outlaw held Gunhill's Winchester one-handed, leaned, and hefted the coffee-pot. It was not quite empty. He growled and Gloryann held up a cup for him to pour, then he tossed the pot aside and took the cup from her, stepped back, carbine aimed, and drank. The coffee was strong and black, and still hot. Afterwards, Webster flung down the cup and gave the girl an order.

"Fill the pot from the creek and pour in more coffee." As she arose to obey, Webster waggled the one-handed carbine. "I'll tell *you* what *he* told me; don't try to outrun a bullet."

She looked at the outlaw with more spirit than Gunhill thought was prudent. Then she said, "I wouldn't run from you, Carl, nor anyone like you." Then she stalked to the creek to re-fill the pot as Webster sank down to sit cross-legged opposite Gunhill. He watched the girl, but he was addressing Gunhill when he said, "You should have stuck to preaching. What made you think I wouldn't hunt you down?"

Gunhill had no ready answer to this, and in fact he'd been feeling disgusted with himself even before Webster spoke, so the only answer he could give, was the one he did give.

"Stupidity, Carl. Just plain stupidity. I have no excuse. In your boots I'd probably have done the same thing — come after a gun and a horse the only place I would have been sure of finding them."

Webster looked at Gunhill, evidently slightly surprised at the unarmed man's candour. "You aren't so damned smart after all," he said, and watched Gloryann return, kneel, and settle the pot upon the stones, then rummage in her saddlebag for the little pouch containing coffee. As she put the aromatic ground beans into the pot, Webster growled at her again.

"Sit down over there beside Gunhill where I can see you both."

She turned towards the outlaw. "You don't want me to feed you?"

Webster wavered, hunger affecting his caution. "All right. Fry me up a meal. But do it on the other side of the fire."

Gloryann continued to kneel, looking at Webster. "I prefer to cook from this side of the fire. I don't like smoke in my eyes." She twisted to dig into the saddlebag again, and Webster's face twisted into a snarling expression, but he hung fire a moment, and that was usually all it took for a man's sudden resentment to dwindle. He watched Gloryann bring food forth, and perhaps the way she went briskly to work completely ignoring him, made Webster give up on her.

He said, "You were right about one thing,

Gunhill; I thought about it out there tonight. I'm going back to Arrow with you. I'm glad you told me Jasper's laid up with a busted leg. That means there'll only be her, and her maw." Webster paused, then smiled. "And you; only you're not going back. You and Tom Jennings are goin' to lie out here for the wolves to find. This time, by gawd, I'll clean out that gawddamned ranch, and when I leave, believe me, no one'll be able to come after me."

Gunhill remained silent, watching Gloryann. He had not pegged Carl Webster as a killer. Perhaps, under some conditions, Webster would kill a man; that applied to just about everyone, outlaw or not, but Gunhill's impressions over this long day as he and Webster had ridden along together, was that the rustler was not a person who shot people out of hand. Jennings *had* impressed Gunhill as that kind of a man, but Webster had not. Now, though, it was beginning to sound as though Gunhill had been wrong about that.

He finally glanced over and said, "Mind if I roll a smoke?"

The outlaw shrugged. "Go ahead. That's what they do for condemned men, isn't it; let 'em have one good meal and a smoke, before they hang 'em?"

Gunhill did not answer. He moved slowly at removing the makings from a shirt-pocket, and in rolling his cigarette. Then he offered the makings to Webster, who shook his head, before pocketing them and leaning to pick up a small firebrand to use in lighting up. As he blew smoke, Gunhill made an observation.

"You'd be a lot smarter to just take your horse, Carl, and lose yourself in the hills."

The outlaw turned scornful. "Would I now? So you could take up my trail? Gunhill, when I ride off this time, nobody's going to be around to trail me. No one at all."

Gunhill gently shook his head at the outlaw. "You won't deliberately kill the girl and her mother."

"Wait," said Webster, "and see whether I'll kill 'em or not."

Gloryann did not raise her eyes from the fry-pan and the fire, but of course she heard everything the two men said to one another, and after the most recent exchange she certainly had to be listening very intently, even though neither of the men more than glanced in her direction, nor acted as though she were around.

She fished in the saddlebag again, and salted the breakfast steak she was cooking, the steak she had brought along for Gunhill's first meal in the ensuing morning. Then she drew the coffeepot over, peered in, dropped in another pinch of something from the little cloth bag in her hand, and afterwards shook the pot before placing it beside the flames again. She stoked up her fire with more twigs, and the flames grew brighter as Gunhill sat and smoked, and gazed in an almost detached manner across at the man with the carbine.

He was mostly silent. There really was not much to say. As long as Carl Webster had the Winchester, it was pointless to try and reason with him, and Gunhill had never been a man who talked just to be talking. He finished the cigarette, dropped it into the fire, met Gloryann's steady, fearless gaze for a moment, and offered a gentle smile.

Webster saw this soundless exchange and growled at them both. "Romantic, you two alone out here on a nice summertime night. Too bad I had to bust in, isn't it?"

Gloryann turned on the outlaw, eyes sparkling. "Carl, you were obnoxious on the ranch. I wasn't sorry to see you leave. You're still obnoxious."

Webster's grip on the Winchester tightened and for a moment Gunhill held his breath. But the outlaw's flash of temper came and went, the grip loosened, and as

Gunhill watched, the outlaw sneered at the girl.

"You should have been nicer to me, back there, Annie."

"Don't you call me Annie!" exclaimed the girl, stiffening, glaring at the outlaw. "If you think I'm afraid of that gun, you're wrong."

Webster's teeth showed in a cruel grin. "It isn't the gun you got to worry about — *Annie!* — it's the bullet that'll come out of it. Now shut your mouth and finish that steak. I'm hungry."

Gunhill, seeing the girl's defiance crystallising for another furious outburst, spoke first. "If you eat, Carl, then take the guns and the horses and head out, you'll have all night to make your getaway, and since it'll take Gloryann and me at least until tomorrow noon to walk to the ranch on foot, you'll be pretty well beyond anyone's reach before sunset tomorrow."

The outlaw's response to this was sarcastic. "Sure nice you got my interests at heart, Gunhill. I sure appreciate havin' someone figure everything out for me like this. And you're plumb right — I could do that; be maybe thirty, forty miles away by tomorrow afternoon. The trouble is — they got money in a strongbox down there. That's where they keep the cash they pay wages with. I'm going down after that — and *then* I'll cut loose all the horses and ride off. No one'll find me that way, either, but I'll have my pockets stuffed with money, and I'll *still* be free. Now, Gunhill, don't you allow that's a better schemes?"

"Depends on what you do after you rob the strongbox," answered Gunhill.

"After . . . ? Oh, you mean about thinnin' out the opposition?"

"Yeah. If you run off the ranch horses, no one can go after you. Jasper can't ride anyway; his leg's splinted and bandaged." Gunhill made a deprecatory gesture. "A girl and an older woman never make much of a threat."

Webster smiled. "You're making yourself out a hero, aren't you? Talking like a Dutch uncle to save the hides of that lousy haft-breed and the womenfolk."

"Robbery, and even rustling and horse-stealing, aren't the same as murder," Gunhill retorted. "Murder is something folks never let go of."

"Is that a damned fact? Gunhill, remember me telling you about a feller getting shot to death over in Idaho during a stage holdup?"

Gunhill remembered, only that slaying had been attributed to Tom Jennings. Now,

Gunhill knew the truth. "You," he said.

Webster inclined his head, just once. "Me. So if you're workin' on my conscience, or something like that, you're wasting your breath."

Gloryann used the same tin plate she'd fed Gunhill on when she slid the breakfast steak out of the fry-pan for Webster. She put it on the grass between them for the outlaw to reach for. She did not fry any more potatoes, although she had a few more which she'd meant to save for their first meal of the coming new day. Then she reached for the coffeepot while Webster grabbed up the plate.

Gunhill waited. If there would be any chance at all to hurl himself across the fire upon the outlaw, it would probably be when he was trying to eat. Cutting steak one-handed, even with a sharp knife, was difficult.

But Webster was already prepared for this; he picked up the steak in one hand, kicked aside the tin plate, kept hold of the cocked Winchester with his right hand, and wolfed down the warm meat without even trying to cut it.

Gloryann watched briefly, then, wearing a look of complete disgust, she put the refilled coffee cup in the grass where she had placed the plate. Then she dried her hands on a cloth and after a slow look over at Gunhill, she got busy scouring the fry-pan for the second time.

She was as silent as a stone. She did not even look at Carl Webster unless she had to. Gunhill wondered what was in her mind. The firelight was bright enough for her face to be adequately limned, but her features were closed down in an impassive way while she worked beside the fire.

Webster had grease on his chin and dripping down the front of his soiled, grass-stained, rumpled shirt. He never took his eyes off Gunhill, which, in a way, was a mark of respect. Even unarmed, Gunhill was dangerous.

Out where the horses had been grazing, they now stood head-hung, sleeping. The cattle, too, were quiet and composed for the long night. A hunting owl swooped low on silent wings, and flapped frantically when he inadvertently shot forth from round the nearest rearward hill and blundered near the firelight.

Gloryann filled a second cup with coffee and held it out for Gunhill. Their eyes met again, their fingers touched, she smiled at him gently, as though to say whatever happened, she was glad they were together.

He brought up his slower smile, and for a moment after taking the cup, he clung to her fingers. He squeezed and she squeezed back; they exchanged something this way, a kind of mutual acknowledgement of things felt but never mentioned, and there was now an excellent chance they would never *be* mentioned, either, and yet they both seemed to want the other one to know.

Carl Webster saw none of this. It transpired in a moment. He was ravenously gnawing on the steak, holding the carbine the same way he'd been holding it since he'd snatched at the meat.

14

When Webster had finished eating, he made a smoke, and Gunhill noticed for the first time that he favoured his left hand, or his left arm. At the time, it meant nothing. Gunhill would not have commented on it, in any case, if Gloryann, putting the fry-pan aside, hadn't also noticed, and spoke up.

"Are you hurt, Carl?"

The outlaw did not deign to reply until he had finished his cigarette, then, as he fished in a shirt-pocket for the match, left-handed, he said, "Fell on a gawddamned jagged rock when I was running up through the forest couple hours back. Cut my arm, but I wrapped it and it's all right, so if you figure that's going to be in your favour —"

"In my favour," exclaimed Gloryann, each word solidly scornful. "I asked because it's natural for people to be helpful."

"Yeah," growled the outlaw. "*Real* helpful. You and that stone-faced son of a bitch over there'd do anything to catch me off-guard. Annie, you're not going to help me."

Webster eased the arm down to his lap. In that position it seemed as sound as the right arm. Gunhill shook his head in silence, and that annoyed Webster too.

"What's wrong with you, Gunhill?"

"Nothing's wrong with me, Webster. All she was offering to do was lend a hand."

"Yeah? And grab the carbine when she was close enough? Do I look like I come down in the last rain?"

Gunhill sighed. "Forget it." Then he stared squarely at Webster and said, "Get it over with, will you? You've eaten and rested — now get the rest of it over with and get the hell on your way."

Webster, his lips parted to snarl, hung there nonplussed. He had said what he intended to do; he had made it amply clear he meant to commit murder. What kind of a person urged another person to kill them? Finally, lacking anything better to say, the outlaw turned to Gloryann, turned back to Gunhill, and smoked through an interval of quiet silence before speaking again.

"You *are* a lousy preacher, aren't you? You're like the rest of them; got some crazy idea about salvation and that bunch of crap. You know something, Gunhill? You're as loco as a Crow medicineman I seen some cowmen hang one time when I was a kid. That silly old bastard stood there in his stinkin' old blanket waving a hawk wing in front of his face mumbling a bunch of sing-song gibberish. When they set him on the horse, yanked off his blanket and took the buzzard's wing or whatever it was, away from him, he closed his eyes and commenced singing real loud in an off-key, nasal way that put a man's nerves on edge. They told him to shut up, then they tied a rag over his mouth and yanked him up. He kicked like a mule for a minute or two, then he just swung, up there, round one way, then back round the other way. And you know something, Gunhill? I was watching real close; nothing come out of him and went sailing up to heaven. He was just another unwashed, dead damned In'ian. You're goin' out the same way — just another dead damned louse." Webster's lips curled cruelly downward. "Salvation! Guys like you turn my stomach. You want salvation?" Webster raised the cocked Winchester a little and wig-wagged with it. "*This* is salvation. Right here on the ground, with the trees and grass all around, and that's all there is to it."

Gloryann kept staring. Webster saw this

and snarled at her. "You'll find out soon enough, Annie."

Gunhill had a dry remark to make. "And *you* called *me* a preacher. What are you trying to do, Carl, convince *yourself,* or convince me?"

Webster yawned, moved his left arm slightly, and seemed to be considering a retort to Gunhill when the girl said, "I've got some clean cloth and medicine in my other saddlebag, Carl."

Webster looked at her. "What *don't* you have in them bags, Annie?"

She did not answer. Instead, she explained about the things she had brought. "Jasper had an idea that if Phil found the cattle, and the thieves who had stolen them, there might be need for bandages and medicine. That's all."

"Jasper thinks of everything, don't he?" sneered the outlaw, and struggled to hold back another yawn. "Well; we'll see what else Jasper has thought of when I ride in, down there. Now you go out and saddle the horses, Annie. We're going up a canyon I know of before I head for the ranch."

Probably Gloryann did not get the implication, but Gunhill did; gunshots in a narrow canyon made sounds that carried straight upwards; the sounds did not spread far and wide, the way they would in open or semi-open country.

As Gloryann arose to depart, she looked at Gunhill, and smiled again. He did not feel like smiling back, but he did so, and after she had gone he said, "Carl, don't hurt the girl."

"No? Leave her to fetch a posse after me?"

"Damn it, she couldn't get a posse in time and you know it. There's no one at the ranch but Jasper, and he's laid up with a busted leg, otherwise she'd have to ride thirty miles to Crow's Landing to find the law and come back with a posse. They couldn't find you even if you rode at a walk. Leave her be."

"Being heroic again, Gunhill?"

"No; at least I'm not trying to be, I just don't want the girl hurt."

"You like her, do you?"

Gunhill's anger was rising, and with it a feeling of recklessness; if he was going to die anyway, he would do better to die trying, rather than just sitting his saddle meekly resigned to a bullet in the back. "I like her," he confessed. "Sure, I like her. She's pretty and she's nice and she's considerate. But most of all, she's only twenty years old, and she's already had her share of bad luck."

Carl Webster gazed out where Gloryann was talking her way up to the nearest horse. In a soft voice he said, "She's pretty all right. I noticed that couple months back when I first signed on with the Arrow outfit. She's pretty as a speckled bird. Me'n Tom talked about that. I had a notion to take her along when we hid out, and commenced making our pick of the steers, but Tom got mad, so I let it slide . . . Maybe you're right, Gunhill. Maybe she's too pretty to shoot. Maybe, this time, I'll just take her along with me." Webster's eyes swung back. "Maybe I'll take her along — and just leave you out there with Tom, for the wolves." When he finished speaking, the outlaw yawned again, then shook his head. "Damn it; coffee's supposed to keep a man awake. I reckon all that supper turned me drowsy, like a snake in a nest of baby mice."

Gunhill had eaten more food and drunk more coffee, and his only reaction had been a temporary feeling of lethargy for a short while after supper. Watching the outlaw, now, he rationalised Webster's condition on the grounds that Webster had not only just eaten, but he had been a long time before that without rest, under tension, and finally, it seemed that Webster did not have the kind of durability most rangemen had; he looked to Gunhill as though he were losing steam, fast, and that was encouraging. Gunhill decided to cause as much delay as he could, he also decided to watch Webster very closely. Without a doubt, once he was ahorseback with the killer herding him up some narrow canyon, his last chance would be gone.

He kept the topic of Gloryann Spencer going. It was the only topic he could think of that the outlaw might not tire off. "If you take her along, you're going to have to stay awake all the time, and you won't be able to turn your back or let down your guard, Carl."

Webster's face froze with antagonism. "You aren't smart, damn it all. I know what you're trying to do — talk me into leaving her run loose."

Gunhill reached up slowly to his pocket for the tobacco sack and papers, as he retorted. "Well; do you blame me? I don't want any harm to come to her." He brought forth the makings and went to work. As he finished, he dangled the sack in an outstretched hand, but Webster did not take it, he said, "You roll me one."

As Gunhill went to work troughing the wheatstraw paper and spilling in the tobacco, he formulated his plan; it was not in the least subtle, and as long as the rustler had that Winchester cocked and aimed across the dying fire, it was not even a very good plan, but it was the only idea he could come up with, so he braced himself to try it.

He lit the smoke, carefully laid the other cigarette in the grass, then leaned with the cigarette held head-high. When Webster bent from the waist, Gunhill exploded. He knew where the carbine barrel was without looking down. His left hand swung fast, palm out. The moment it contacted steel, the iciness of that cold metal flashed through him like an electrical shock. One second later, Webster's desperate and spasmodic yank on the trigger blew the night-hush apart with a deafening crash of sound. The gunbarrel was inches past Gunhill's side. He thought for half a second he could feel the tug of steel passing through his coat, then he was hurtling across the fire, and Webster was reacting with the same kind of instantaneous reflexes, scrambling backward, trying to roll clear.

Gunhill pawed cloth, flesh, then night air as the outlaw got clear and spun half around to claw up to his feet. Gunhill's momentum helped; he was able to hit the ground, both booted feet in the fire, which was scattered wildly, bright coals showering around in the grass, as he dug in and shot straight upright. He did not dare allow Webster the two seconds he would need to lever the Winchester, and another couple of seconds to whirl and fire, so he slammed down hard, propelling himself straight at the moving cow-thief. They collided, hard, and Webster, who did not really have himself untracked yet, stumbled, then he sought desperately to swing the carbine, not as a weapon this time as much as a club. The blow struck Gunhill on one thigh and glanced away.

Webster's breath burst forth in a ripped-out curse as he tried to jump away and haul the carbine back for another clubbing strike. Gunhill pressed him too fast and too close. Webster still had the gun rising when an outstretched arm jammed him hard, pushing him off-balance still further.

Webster let go of the rifle and tried to spring to one side, grabbing frantically for his hip-holster. Gunhill reached him with a stinging left fist, half turning him away again. Then he caught the outlaw's left sleeve and wrenched hard, hauling the outlaw back around so that he could grope desperately for Webster's right wrist as it moved upwards with the holstered gun in a tight grip. They rocked together, faces only inches apart, breath coming in expolsive gasps, neither one able to force the other man back. Webster's right arm was pinned to his side by Gunhill's left hand. Webster raised his left hand with the fingers talon-curled, seeking his adversary's eyes. Gunhill dropped his face into the outlaw's shirt-front, swung his right low, as hard as he could, and sunk it wrist-deep, twice, in the cow-thief's soft middle. The second time Webster gasped, yielded one backward step and threw all his body backwards in an attempt to break Gunhill's hold on his gun-wrist.

They fell, Gunhill on top, and this time, when the outlaw groped murderously for Gunhill's eyes with his claw-curled fingers, Gunhill was able to knock the arm upwards, away, and hauled back his right hand, but when Webster saw the cocked fist, he arched his entire body to throw Gunhill off, and at the same time, swung his face as far to one side as he could.

Gunhill's fist struck grass and earth. Pain went up his arm like a hot stab of flame all the way to the shoulder. He threw all his weight to the left, pinning that gunhand to the ground, hauled back to sledge in another blow, and this time when the outlaw tried to anticipate it by jerking his head away,

Gunhill was ready. His fist grated over flesh and cheekbone and up across Webster's face into the hair at his temple.

The outlaw's arched body hung stiffened and strained for a moment, then gradually loosened down to a limp flatness against the ground. His wide-sprung eyes glazed momentarily.

Gunhill eased up enough to grope for the sixgun, wrench it clear and pitch it out into the night. He caught the outlaw by the shirt-front, reared back, and they both came up off the ground.

Webster was not an easy man to put down and keep down. He struggled, without much coordination and without actually seeming to be in control of himself, but he still pushed and pulled and pawed at his adversary, until Gunhill shoved him off two feet, turned his body in behind his right fist, sank both feet hard down, and fired from the shoulder.

Webster's head snapped back, his body bowed over backwards, his arms flopped in mid-air, then he didn't fall as much as he sailed away, struck on his back and slid in the dewy grass to a lengthwise stop, flat and seemingly lifeless.

Gunhill's lungs felt as though they were on fire. He stood above the unconscious man gulping down great draughts of air, waiting, but Carl Webster had nothing left in him; even had he been conscious, he wouldn't have had much left in him, but Gunhill did not know the reason for this, yet.

A small, cold hand stole into Gunhill's swelling right fist, the icy fingers entwining. Gloryann moved so close they touched at hip and shoulder, and stared, solemn as an owl, at the battered, bloody-mouthed unconscious outlaw in the night-sooted grass.

She said, "He's dead, Phil."

Gunhill did not answer. He knew better; he had hit Webster with everything he had, but it hadn't been enough of a blow to break the man's neck. The main reason he did not answer, though, was because as he stood there, sore and aching and spent, he did not care to tell her that he did not give a damn whether the man was dead or not.

15

They dragged Carl Webster closer to the fire where Gloryann compassionately sponged off his face with a cloth soaked with cold creekwater. Then, after a few minutes, Gunhill knelt down and tied the outlaw's arms behind him, rolled him onto his stomach, ran the rope on down, and lashed his legs fast at the ankles as well.

Gloryann brought the ivory-handled Colt and dropped it into Gunhill's holster as he was working on their vanquished enemy. She leaned, looked, then said, "You didn't have to do that."

Gunhill looked up quizzically. "Do what? Jump him?"

"Yes. He would have passed out in another few minutes."

Gunhill knelt astraddle the unconscious, limp form, staring upwards.

"I was watching him from out by the horses," explained the girl. "He would have toppled over in another few minutes. Remember when I shook the coffee pot? Well, I poured some of the medicine from the little bottle Jasper had me fetch along, into the coffee."

"What was in the bottle?"

"Laudanum, Phil. Jasper said I should bring it with the other bandage-cloth and medicine. He thought that if you found those outlaws, there would be a fight, and he thought that when I found you, you might need something. Maybe a pain-deadener like laudanum."

Gunhill sank back on his heels staring at the unconscious outlaw. "*That's* why he kept yawning."

"Yes. You and he were arguing when I poured about a third of the bottle into the coffee. Neither one of you even looked at me when I did it." Gloryann leaned, took hold of Phil's right hand and raised it in the rusty moonlight for a close inspection. The knuckles were bruised and swelling, but Gunhill was already satisfied nothing was broken. He let her hold the hand, and when she looked at him, he was half smiling and looking straight back. She released the hand and stepped back a little.

"You can't do any crochetting with that hand for a week," she said, and smiled.

She had to practically re-kindle the fire; his lunge across at the outlaw had scattered ash and coals. Then she re-arranged the stone-ring and made another pot of coffee. As she worked, Gunhill crossed over where he had been before the fight, kicked some hot coals farther away into the dew-speckled green grass, and dropped down. Miraculously, the cigarette he had placed so carefully in the grass was still lying there, damp, but otherwise uninjured.

He put it aside, closer to the stone-ring where heat would dry the paper, then he flexed his right hand, watching it, as he said, "We're going to have to develop some kind of separate signals, or maybe converse in Athabascan or something. Otherwise you're going to be doing things right, and I'm going to be blundering along, duplicating your efforts in my incorrect and clumsy fashion."

He looked up when he finished speaking, and slowly grinned across the fire at her. She said, "What did he mean about you being a preacher?"

"Well; I studied for the ministry for about a year after the war. But I didn't finish. A man I worked with knew me better than I knew myself. He saved me from making a pretty embarrassing mistake."

"You'd have made a splendid minister, Phil."

He had a little trouble plumbing that; if it was intended as a compliment, then of course he was pleased, if it was one of those oblique compliments, like telling a man he would make a good laundress because his hands were too small to hold a pitchfork, then he wasn't pleased.

She laughed at the expression on his face. "You really would have have. You have a nice voice, your grammar is much better than the grammar of most cowboys I've known, and you look — well, dignified. You inspire confidence in people."

He said, "You'd better quit. My hat's beginning to shrink. It couldn't be that my head's getting too big for it, I'm sure of that."

She sank back on her heels across the fire from him.

"I would have helped in the fight. I had your gun, but I was afraid to fire. I might have hit you, instead of Carl."

He was very glad she hadn't gotten carried away; it was bad enough being cowed by one's own Winchester, but it was much worse being shot by one's own Colt. In expressing this idea, though, he made a mistake.

"Just as well you didn't. A sixgun is a man's weapon."

She rocked back and forth gazing steadily at him for a moment, then leaned and held out a hand, palm up. "May I see the gun again, please?"

He had no objection. As he passed the heavy sixgun over, she picked up a stone from the fire-ring, pitched it into the air, flashed his gun in a tilting position and fired. Gunhill jumped. The stone broke into a dozen fragments.

Gunhill was annoyed. Anyway, it had been a pure accident. The stone was dark, the night was darker. Hitting a flying target under those circumstances, even for a man who was experienced, would have been a very chancy thing. He held out his hand for the gun, showing disapproval.

She did not hand him the gun, instead she picked up another stone and lay it upon his palm. "Throw it up."

He almost refused, but if she needed a lesson in humility, he was not the slightest bit averse to seeing that she got it. Gunhill leaned back and hurled the stone. As it sailed upwards, it began to spin away sidewards. The gun flashed orange, the explosion shattered the night for the second time, and with Gunhill watching, the stone suddenly took an immense upwards, tumbling impetus, then it broke the way the previous stone had done, fragments falling back to earth.

She punched out the pair of spent casings, reversed the sixgun and placed it gently upon his hand. "I wouldn't have missed Carl, if I'd aimed at him."

Gunhill punched up two casings from his shellbelt, wordlessly re-loaded the Colt, bolstered it and reached for one of the tin cups because the coffeepot was shudderings as its contents boiled. He did not say a word.

She filled his cup first, then filled one for herself, and with a perplexed gaze, watched his face. He still said nothing, not even after he'd tasted the scalding coffee and had lowered the cup to the grass at his side.

She changed expression, began to seem worried and apprehensive. "Phil?"

"Yes?"

"I'm sorry."

He gave her a level look. "For what?"

"Well; I didn't mean to be a show-off."

"Most people don't mean to be — when they are," he told her. "Too bad your father didn't have a boy to teach things like that to."

She agreed. "Yes."

"And while we're on the subject, most

men don't like a woman to try and do their talking and thinking for them."

"Yes. But after my father died, and after Jasper got hurt —"

"They *still* don't like it," he exclaimed. "I don't care what the circumstances are."

"Yes."

He loosened a little. "I thought that was a lucky shot, when you hit the cougar from that distance."

She did not even hesitate. "Believe me, it *was* a lucky shot. Would you like the rest of the coffee?"

He wouldn't. All he really wanted now was about fifteen hours of uninterrupted sleep, but he wasn't going to get it. It was now about midnight, he thought, and they would be in the saddle again at dawn making the final drive to the ranch, so even if he fell over right now and slept hard, he still was not going to get more than about four hours of slumber.

He arose, went out to the saddles, yanked loose two bedrolls, his and hers, brought them back and tossed one across the fire at her feet.

He shucked his gunbelt, unrolled his blankets with his back to her, sat down to kick off his boots, and without looking across the fire, he heard her also getting ready to climb into her blankets. He sat a moment, then said, "Did you hear *all* we said, after you went out to the horses?"

"Yes."

He looked over. She was already inside her bedroll, a blanket pulled up under her chin, her curly head turned slightly so that she could see him opposite her, her violet eyes black in the firelight.

Gunhill cleared his throat. "Well; you see, I had to keep him talking, keep him diverted as much as possible."

"Then you didn't mean all those — things?"

Gunhill looked over where the outlaw was slumbering. "You sure must have given him quite a jolt of that laudanum."

"Phil; you didn't mean those things?"

He arose in his stockinged feet. "I'd better bring over a couple of the saddleblankets; be a heck of a note if he caught pneumonia and you had to look after him for a month at the ranch before you could take him to the law over at Crow's Landing."

"Phil . . . ?"

He went out, shook out a pair of double blankets, returned, stepping gingerly, and held both blankets to the fire until they were adequately warmed, then he arranged them over Carl Webster.

"Phil . . . ?"

He got back to his bedroll and sat down again. "If you're worrying about when we'll reach the ranch . . ." He raised his legs, eased inside the clammy bedroll, and very slowly stretched out his full length. "It's up to you. We can drift the steers right on into the corrals behind the barn, for Jasper to look over before they're turned out, or we can drift them down another two or three miles, then let them fan out, and ride on in by ourselves. It's plumb up to you."

She raised her head and propped it upon one arm. "For a man who doesn't seem to like trivial talk, Phil Gunhill, you've certainly been spreading a lot of it around this past half hour. I asked you a question."

"Go to sleep."

"No!"

"Well then, just lie there and count stars. I'm tired."

"I'm not going to let you go to sleep until you've answered my question."

He dropped flat, rolled up onto his side, his back to her, and emitted a great groan. "And that's another thing men don't like about women — being pig-headed."

"You don't like me anyway," she retorted, "so I can't make things any worse if I keep you awake."

He agreed with part of that. "No, you can't make things any worse, but you sure as the devil can end up getting bent over my knee and paddled."

"What did you say? You wouldn't dare!"

He lay a moment looking out across the grass towards the drowsing horses, then he groaned again, pitched half upright in his blankets, twisted and aimed a finger at her. "You go to sleep. At least be quiet, or you're going to find out whether I'll dare paddle you or not. Annie; stop asking that question, too."

They remained propped up staring across the little fire for a long moment, then she smiled slowly and said, "All right. I'm sorry," and leaned to pick up a handful of twigs and throw them on the fire. As he dropped back down, making his third groan within the past ten minutes, she lay back with the firelight climbing again, sending warmth out to them both, and she did as he'd suggested earlier, she looked up, counting stars. He hadn't said he *hadn't* meant those things he'd told Webster about her. He hadn't said he *had* meant them either, but if a man refused to deny something, then at least *part* of it was probably true.

She would settle for that, and with a soft-tender smile she closed her eyes, body loose and warm and comfortable inside the bed-roll, until a terrible sound brought her straight up. Gunhill was snoring!

She waited a moment until her heartbeat was back to normal, then she turned — and hung there a moment, until the natural sensation of indignation had passed — and finally she lay back again, half-smiling, and closed her eyes to sleep.

16

Two sounds awakened Gunhill, one was the movement and lowing of cattle freshly risen from their beds and hungry, and the second sound was the anguished profanity of Carl Webster.

Gunhill sat up, looked around, saw the sun off in the east barely clear of a rim, saw the empty bedroll across the way, glanced quickly out where the horses were — and saw her at the creek filling the small coffeepot.

The horses were already grazing. Even their little cooking-fire was smoking from a fresh load of kindling. Gunhill hauled up out of his blankets, pulled on his boots, dropped the hat upon the back of his head and went over to partially untie Webster. He helped the outlaw sit up, then he propped him in that position, looked at the swollen, discoloured face, and shook his head.

"You look like a head of cabbage after a

black frost," he told Webster. "You're a mess."

"I got the damndest headache a man ever had," complained the outlaw. "What the hell did you hit me with?"

Gunhill straightened up and, without answering, headed for the creek. When he got down there, Gloryann was among the horses, looking them over. Gunhill flung down his hat and knelt to wash — there in the grass was a towel and a cake of soap. He picked up the soap; she had thought of everything. Or maybe women just naturally went everywhere packing towels and soap.

The water was like a stinging slap in the face. It very effectively dissolved the last cobweb inside Gunhill's head. He couldn't shave, but that was not to be helped, so, as he went back to the breakfast fire, where Gloryann was sitting on her heels at work, he rubbed his jaw a little self-consciously, then smiled when she raised her eyes. "No razor," he said.

Her answer was forthright. "You'd look distinguished with a beard, Phil."

From behind her a short distance, Webster snorted. "You'd look better with a rope around your gullet," he told Gunhill, who ignored the prisoner and sat crosslegged across from Gloryann.

She looked very young in the soft, newday sunshine. Cold creekwater had given her cheeks and throat a pink shading. She was wearing a fresh blouse, which she rounded out with a proud and muscular thrust. She had managed to comb her hair, until it shone like new copper, with dark gold streaks. In Gunhill's eyes she was both boyishly lithe and strong, and girlishly willowy and rounded. It was a very disturbing combination, especially in the eyes of a man who had not been around women, out of choice, for a very long while.

Nor could Gunhill erase from his mind the personal things they had talked about — or *argued* about — the night before.

She seemed to be more inward this morning than she had been the previous day, or last night. She seemed to be hugging close some satisfactory secret. She did not try to force a conversation with Gunhill, and she did not actually look up at him, unless it was necessary. The only time she spoke forth at any length was when she explained about their morning meal.

"I didn't bring enough for three people, and last night when we fed Carl, that meat was supposed to be for your breakfast and mine. I've had to cut up the last of the steaks into three pieces. They're small shares."

He leaned to look into the fry-pan. They were indeed small pieces, and there were no more of those fried spuds, but Gunhill was nowhere nearly as hungry this morning as he had been the night before.

He tended the coffee, took a cup back to Carl, who grumbled about his headache again, and asked Gunhill to roll him a cigarette. After this was done, and Gunhill had also held the light for Carl, the outlaw shot him a sceptical look and said, "I feel like I been on a weeklong drunk. Damn you anyway, Gunhill."

Gloryann brought over Webster's tin plate. The outlaw had his arms free, but his ankles were still tied. He accepted the plate with a sullen glare at the girl, until Gunhill leaned and tapped his shoulder. Then the outlaw said, "Thanks, Annie."

She flared at him. "I told you not to call me Annie. The next time I'm going to slap you so hard you'll —"

"That's what your paw used to call you," snapped the headachy outlaw.

"Yes," she agreed. "And so does Phil call me that — sometimes. But not *you.* Not anyone like you."

She arose and returned to the fire, keeping her back to them both. Webster looked up. "You want some advice?" he asked Gunhill, who was standing there admiring the girl. "I'll give it to you anyway; don't even think about climbing into double harness with that one. She'd make a man's life plumb miserable. Don't know her place. That's her trouble. Bossy, talks back, thinks she knows it all . . ." Webster lowered his head and started eating his breakfast.

Gunhill returned to the fire, filled another cup of coffee and when Gloryann offered him the second plate he said, "You'd better make another pot of coffee. This thing's about empty." Then he waited.

She arose without a murmur and went down to the creek with the coffeepot. Webster sat over there staring.

There was no need for haste, now, so Gunhill took his time about eating, and afterwards, about striking camp, getting his two prisoners, the dead one and the living one, tied to their horses. He helped Gloryann roll their blankets and stow their camp gear. He saddled her horse while she was doing other things, and when they met she smiled at him and said, "You're the first person, except my father, I've ever worked with who didn't have to figure out which each one of us would do." She swung up into the saddle and waited for him to take the lead.

Webster assumed his old role as caretaker of the lead-horse with its grisly burden, and he did it as sullenly as he could have been expected to do it. His headache had diminished considerably, but he still ached from the shellacking he'd received in his fight the night before. But a man could live with physical aches; rangemen were seldom free of that kind of inconvenience.

The cattle resented being grouped and headed out; they were back in familiar territory and had no wish to be pushed deeper into it. But they went, and Gunhill chose the route.

The morning was golden and summer-scented. A lot had happened, and there was still more that *would* happen, but Gunhill was satisfied that the worst was over and done with.

He rode slouched and easy. When Gloryann drifted back to ride stirrup with him, they discussed the cattle, mostly, and Jasper's reaction to what they had to tell him. Then Gunhill mentioned, once again, something she had avoided when he'd asked it previously.

He said, "How is your ankle?"

She had probably come to some kind of

decision concerning this, last night. At least, this time, she did not act evasive.

"It wasn't sprained nor broken. It *did* hurt like the dickens though, when I fell."

"And the cracked ribs?"

She looked at him, eyes wide, lips ruefully curled. "Do you have to be so inquisitive?"

He kept a perfectly straight face. "No."

With true womanly logic she then said, "In that case I'll tell you. My ankle *did* hurt. It wasn't broken or anything like that, and I knew it while I was sitting there after the horse fell with me. But . . . the idea came to me when you offered to help me up."

"What idea?"

"Well. Darn you, do you simply *have* to know?"

Gunhill looked out over the swaying red backs of the steers and ran a hand over his scratchy jaw. "I reckon not."

She studied his profile, then blurted it out. "I didn't want you to leave."

He nodded gently, still looking away from her, out at the ambling steers. "I wondered."

"You don't have to wonder any more, then."

He turned and glanced down. "I didn't really want to leave. While I was nooning up there, before you came out of the trees like a herd of wild horses, I was thinking about you . . . When you showed up, I was surprised, but I wasn't sorry."

She evened up the reins in her hands with meticulous care, studying each rein separately as she said, "I was in the chicken-run. I heard you and Jasper talking. I — didn't want you to go, but I couldn't think of a single thing to say to make you stay. Then, after you'd ridden out, I saddled up and loped parallel to you . . . I didn't know that calvy heifer was out there, but when I saw her, knew what her trouble was, I'd already seen you, so I decided to rope the heifer and call on you to help me . . . It didn't work out that way." She stopped adjusting the reins and shot him a look. "It worked even better. But I still had to come up with something; the sore ankle gave me the idea." She shot him another sidelong glance. "That wasn't honest at all, was it?"

No, it hadn't been honest, but Gunhill knew something about women, about the innate *character* of women; they were not large nor muscular, and regardless of what people said about the world belonging to the intelligent and not to the strong, it was not true. At least it was *rarely* true. Women had to use methods to achieve their ends, sometimes, that weren't strictly honest. He didn't know much more than that, but knowing *that* was more than a great many men knew, who had been around women much more than Gunhill had.

He said, "Sure a nice day, isn't it?" and when she looked quizzically at him, his slow smile came. She smiled more swiftly, more spontaneously, it was like a flash of light and warmth, it transformed her entire face.

"I like you, Mr Gunhill," she said. "Do you know why?"

"Sure; because I'm cute."

She stiffened for a moment, then rolled in the saddle laughing. If there was one thing a burly, powerful, rough, battling-type of a man was *not,* it was cute. In fact, Gunhill was not even handsome. He was nice-looking, had fine eyes and a generous, humorous mouth, but otherwise he was not outstanding — except in a way that did not show.

When she stopped laughing, he said, "I like you too. Tell you what, Annie; if your mother'll allow it, I'll adopt you. I'd like to have a daughter just like —"

She hooked her horse with savage suddenness and raced away. Webster, drowsing along farther back, roused himself to stare, and to frown in bafflement. He called ahead.

"What the hell did you do, Gunhill? What did you say to her?"

Gunhill, head tilted, watching the distant rider, answered without taking his eyes off Gloryann as she went flinging down the far side of the ambling steers.

"Shut up, Carl."

"You're clumsy," stated the outlaw, also looking far ahead. "That's your trouble, you're clumsy with womenfolk."

"I said shut up!"

"She likes you. Hell, even the horses can sense that. And you're like a cub bear handling an icicle — all thumbs."

Gunhill turned and reined his horse back, waiting for Webster to come up abreast of him. The outlaw's badly swollen, discoloured and lopsided face showed all the ravages of his last beating by Gunhill. Webster eyed his captor with cynical eyes. "You aren't going to hit me," he told Gunhill. "And I don't have to shut up . . . You can roll me a smoke, though."

Gunhill made them both a cigarette, lit both and shoved one at the outlaw. Webster inhaled deeply, let grey smoke trickle out, shook his head and said, "You're a good man with guns and fists, and even with tracks and livestock, Gunhill. I know your kind — a tophand. But around womenfolk . . ." Webster dolorously wagged his head and kept right on wagging it until

Gunhill became so irritated he pushed his horse on ahead. By then, they were in sight of the ranch, of the sunlighted buildings in their picturesque primeval setting.

There were three people far ahead. One of them had a thick, stiff, white leg stuck out in front. He was leaning on a gnarled walking stick.

Gunhill gestured for someone down there to open the corral gates. Immediately, the lean, lithe, coppery-headed distant figure holding a horse, swung up and reined away to obey.

Webster saw this and had another comment to make. "But you got a knack for gettin' them to work like a good cowdog, Gunhill. I'll give you that. You do it with hand-signals, just like a man does with the best cowdogs."

Gunhill stared at Carl Webster; that kind of a comparison would never have crossed his mind.

17

Gloryann was at the main-house with her mother. Gunhill and Carl Webster sat on the bunkhouse porch in the nooning sunlight with Jasper, and the fourth man was in the back of a battered wagon inside the cool barn, freshly wrapped in some old, stained canvas.

Jasper had heard most of the story from Gloryann before Gunhill reached the yard. Then he had heard the rest of it from Gunhill, while they had stood atop that little hill southeast of the ranch where Gloryann's father had been buried, while they watched Carl Webster dig and swear and sweat profusely, until he had the grave deep enough, and finally, while the three of them rested a moment or two before hauling Tom Jennings out to his grave, Gunhill and Webster told Jasper all that remained to be told — except for one thing: Gunhill did not mention the interlude between himself and

Gloryann.

Webster could have said something. He did not know it all, but he knew some of it. But Webster had much more critical things on his mind. One of them had to do with the leg-iron Jasper had produced, from over in the smithy, and which now lay ominously upon the bunkhouse porch.

It was Jasper himself who brought up that matter of Gunhill and Gloryann when he said, somewhat dryly and mildly, that the girl's recovery from being injured during the jerk-down was the fastest and most complete recovery he had ever seen.

Gunhill slouched in porch-shade gazing out across the yard, saying nothing. Webster, smoking and resting, was also silent on this matter.

Jasper allowed a moment to pass before speaking again. "Bad enough to turn out wrong about men; you figure you know riders after you've been round them a month or two — like Carl and Tom — then it turns out you didn't know 'em at all. That's bad enough. But I've been around Gloryann since the first few months after the Spencers settled in, up here. I'd have bet money I could predict her. Damned if I didn't turn up wrong about that too."

Gunhill shifted slightly in his chair, but

continued to be silent, and to gaze distantly across the sun-drenched, dramatically picturesque range country.

Jasper put his black gaze upon Gunhill. "I sort of had you figured, too."

Gunhill sighed. "You were wrong, Jasper."

"Was I?"

"Yeah. I had to bring her back. She was hurt. At least I thought she was hurt, and couldn't make it by herself. But I didn't have to stay."

"You didn't like the idea of Carl and Tom taking advantage of the women."

Gunhill shrugged thick shoulders. "Maybe. You're partly right; I didn't like that. But you said it yourself — losing fifty steers wouldn't bankrupt them; they'd pull through just fine."

"Then why did you go after them, Gunhill?"

"Well, because of the girl. I couldn't shake her out of my mind." Gunhill turned, smiling. "So you see, you were wrong again."

Jasper chuckled. "That's just it, Gunhill. That's just exactly what I privately figured about you. *I was right.* I watched you lead her back to the ranch after she got jerked down, I watched you help her off the horse over at the main-house, and I told myself you'd stay on . . . Well, I don't blame you.

She's as pretty as a picture and she's handy."

"Bossy," muttered Webster. "She's one of them women who's always got to try and compete with men; she thinks she's as smart, as wise, as strong —" Webster shook his head. "Gunhill, if you take my advice, you'll ride out of here and never even look back."

Gunhill arose slowly, eased his hat forward to shade his eyes and stepped down off the porch. "Let's plant Jennings and get that over with."

The three of them went down to the wagon, climbed in, Jasper at the lines, and soberly drove the rig over to the new grave. Webster and Gunhill lowered the canvas-wrapped corpse and while Jasper intoned the fragments of some prayers he'd learned as a youngster, the other two piled in the dirt. Afterwards, mounding and shaping the grave, Webster said, "Well, it don't last too long, even at its best, does it?" and Gunhill gazed at the outlaw who had tried to kill him, who had broken every law he could, and would have broken more if that had been possible, and shook his head.

"If you don't learn from his mistakes, Carl, you're going to end up the same way." He wasn't trying to preach, he was stating his conviction.

They trooped back to the wagon and drove down to the yard, to the barn, where Gunhill put up the horse while Webster parked the wagon, then Jasper herded the outlaw over to the bunkhouse to be leg-ironed until someone had the time to deliver him to the law at Crow's Landing, while Gunhill went out back to scrub and shave, and lean in afternoon sunlight for a few minutes, thinking, smoking, making a careful judgement and arriving at a thought-out decision.

He was still back there in the late-day shadows and fragrance when Gloryann came round the side of the log building, freshly scrubbed, freshly dressed, her curly copper-gold hair shades darker in the shadows. She paused and looked up, then smiled and moved in a little closer.

"Jasper said you were back here." She leaned upon the rough log wall. "Are you tired, Phil?"

He *was* tired. He was also getting hungry. But he did not admit to either. "We buried Jennings."

She nodded. "My mother and I saw you go out with the wagon and come back later." She did not take her eyes off his face. "There's a full moon tonight."

"Is there?"

"Do you like to ride on full-moon nights?"

He leaned, dropped the cigarette, stamped on it and smiled at her. "Yes."

"Tonight, then, after supper?"

"Is this what you want, Annie?"

"Yes."

He stepped over, opened his arms, and she walked in very close and raised up onto her tip-toes, small, brown hands lying lightly upon his chest. She sought his mouth and when he kissed her, what started out to be an almost brotherly embrace, suddenly became something almost totally overpowering for them both. She clung to him, full length, his arms locked round her, when his needs and hungers flared, she responded with similar needs and hungers.

When they slackened off, she hid her face from him, and he still held her against him, looking westward down across the distance towards some far-away, blurry hills, satisfied that the decision he had made was the right one for them both. He would stay.

Jasper *had* been right.

ABOUT THE AUTHOR

Lauran Paine who, under his own name and various pseudonyms has written over 900 books, was born in Duluth, Minnesota, a descendant of the Revolutionary War patriot and author, Thomas Paine. His family moved to California when he was at an early age and his apprenticeship as a Western writer came about through the years he spent in the livestock trade, rodeos, and even motion pictures where he served as an extra because of his expert horsemanship in several films starring movie cowboy Johnny Mack Brown. In the late 1930s, Paine trapped wild horses in Northern Arizona and even, for a time, worked as a professional farrier. Paine came to know the Old West through the eyes of many who had been born in the previous century and he learned that Western life had been very different from the way it was portrayed on the screen. "I knew men who had killed other men," he later recalled. "But they were the exceptions. Prior to and during the Depression, people were just too busy eking out an existence to indulge in Saturday-night brawls." He served in the U.S. Navy in the Second World War and began writing for Western pulp magazines following his discharge. It is interesting to note that all of his earliest novels (written under his own name and the pseudonym Mark Carrel) were published in the British market and he soon had as strong a following in that country as in the United States. Paine's Western fiction is characterized by strong plots, authenticity, an apparently effortless ability to construct situation and character, and a preference for building his stories upon a solid foundation of historical fact. *Adobe Empire* (1956), one of his best novels, is a fictionalized account of the last twenty years in the life of trader William Bent and, in an off-trail way, has a melancholy, bittersweet texture that is not easily forgotten. *Moon Prairie* (1950), first published in the United States in 1994, is a memorable story set during the mountain man period of the frontier. In later novels such as *The Homesteaders* (1986) or *The Open Range Men* (1990), he showed that the special magic and power of his stories and characters had only matured along with his basic themes of changing times, changing attitudes, learning from experience, respecting nature, and the yearning for a simpler, more moderate way of life. His most recent Western novels include *Tears of the Heart, Lockwood* and *The White Bird.*

We hope you have enjoyed this Large Print book. Other Thorndike, Wheeler, and Chivers Press Large Print books are available at your library or directly from the publishers.

For information about current and upcoming titles, please call or write, without obligation, to:

Publisher
Thorndike Press
295 Kennedy Memorial Drive
Waterville, ME 04901
Tel. (800) 223-1244

or visit our Web site at:

http://gale.cengage.com/thorndike

OR

Chivers Large Print
published by BBC Audiobooks Ltd
St James House, The Square
Lower Bristol Road
Bath BA2 3SB
England
Tel. +44(0) 800 136919
email: bbcaudiobooks@bbc.co.uk
www.bbcaudiobooks.co.uk

All our Large Print titles are designed for easy reading, and all our books are made to last.